Naked WITH THE NEW JERSEY DEVIL

URBAN LEGEND EROTICA COLLECTION

HONEY CUMMINGS

4 Horsemen
Publications, Inc.

4 Horsemen
Publications, Inc.

Published By: 4 Horsemen Publications, Inc.

4 Horsemen Publications, Inc.
PO Box 417
Sylva, NC 28779
4horsemenpublications.com
info@4horsemenpublications.com

Cover & Typesetting by Valerie Willis

Paperback ISBN-13: 978-1-64450-065-1
Audiobook ISBN-13: 978-164450-052-1
Ebook ISBN-13: 978-1-64450-053-8

DEDICATION

To Kim & Deidre

Your real life stories of Jersey & Philly were quite the inspiration! Stay awesome and keep writing ladies!

XOXO
Honey Cummings

TABLE OF CONTENTS

TAKE ME TO CHURCH

Abigail Montgomery inhaled deeply as she pushed through the church doors. *Why am I so nervous?* Her pastel-toned floral sundress floated behind her as she strode down the center aisleway. The pews were bare, the church a silent tomb. *Not like I'm getting married today.* Her mulatto complexion was a warm contrast to the flowery colors backed in white on the thin fabric. *This is a little lower cut than normal, but it's not like I'm here for Sunday service.*

She'd taken the day off work, hoping to sneak her fiancé, Pastor Bradley O'Malley, lunch. Lately, they were so busy with her long days dealing with a mid-year review and him seeming to be more active with church activities during the weekdays, and sometimes evenings. At times, she couldn't shake the feeling that it all started the night they were going to have sex; something he had started and stopped before making her promise to *save it for our wedding night. I want our first time to be special.*

1

Abigail grimaced. *It's not like either of us are virgins. Maybe he feels he should as a pastor? I should respect that.*

The place was empty as she paused in the center of the main aisle. Her plump lips frowned, her tight curls framing her face as her mahogany brown eyes glance at her phone. *Did I read his text wrong?*

[Abigail: Hey, what are your plans for lunch?]

[BJ: Sorry, Abby. Busy mentoring a congressional member.]

Weird. When did he become a mentor?

Scanning the room, she caught sight of Bradley's Bible, laid open on the podium. Wandering around the pulpit, she closed the cover on the organ keys out of habit. She had enjoyed playing it, learning the songs. *I miss this, but after playing at mom's funeral...* Furrowing her brow, her thoughts redirected, shielding her from her own emotions. It all seemed odd.

He goes nowhere without that book. Even got mad when I touched it once. Where could he be?

The sound of muffled voices brought her attention to the open hallway, to the offices located behind the worship room, in the back half of the building. If he was mentoring at this time, then he must be using his office for private discussion.

Don't they schedule these things in tandem with another Pastor in case someone walks in? It must have been...

Goosebumps rolled over her. The muffled voices turned into moans. Not of pain, but something she knew too well. Abigail tilted her head, her mind racing with speculation. *Is, is someone having sex in the church?* Her heart fluttered; her mouth parched as she bit her lip. She was even with his office door; it was wide open and empty. Halting, she questioned what she should do next. *Is the deacon taking booty calls now?* Forcing her body to continue, the sounds were louder, more erotic. Some part of her felt excited, from imagining the act or perhaps the idea of catching a couple in a lude act in the holiest of places.

It's coming from the private baptism room. Somebody is having a hell of a time. I mean, I used to have some fun at the club like this, but they're in the damn church doing this.

Pressing her palm flat on the door, it cracked open. *How careless, they didn't close it all the way or even bother to lock it.* She pushed slowly and held her breath. *Don't squeak, I just want a peak.* At last, she could see a reflection from a glass case full of keepsakes and novelty items. None of that came into focus as she could see a man's bare backside. Two legs spread wide on either side of him; the woman laid across the receiving table. Abigail licked her lips, swallowing as their grinding came into view.

Who is that? Do I know them? I mean, I think I know most of the congregation.

The legs encircled the man's waist, arms reaching up to him. As the woman arched and her face came into few, Abigail's eyes widened. *Tammy the organ player? That old hag? Really? Who in the hell would go out with her? She has a laugh like Fran Drescher from The Nanny.* Her shoulders shuddered, but... *Still, what a wild sex life she has. I can't say I haven't fantasized about Pastor Bradley and me...* Tammy's moaning interrupted her thoughts.

Abigail leaned too much on the door and it banged against something. She squatted and covered her ears with her hands. *What the hell am I doing?* Removing them, she shot back to the reflection. She could see the rest of him, the muscled ass cheeks and thighs, the pants that had slid to his ankles. *He's got a nice ass! I'm impressed. Though I think he could be working her...*

The man stopped, aiming to turn but Tammy grabbed his shoulder. "Did you hear that?"

"Don't stop. Please, fuck me harder." She begged, panting as she tilted her hips against him.

"Tammy." She forced the man's face back to her. "If we..."

3

She pushed against him, her knees rising higher as they hugged his ribs. "Take me to church, Pastor."

A PASTOR! But which one? Abigail watched the reflection, wondering how long they would continue. *I just want to watch a little longer, see a little more of this pastor who would...*

Her blood ran cold. *It can't be.* A wristwatch glinted in the reflection, and she stood in alarm. Pushing through the door, making a ruckus as chairs toppled over, she laid her eyes directly on the fucking couple, no longer caring about satisfying sexual curiosity. "B-Bradley?"

He swiveled his head around, locking his blue eyes with hers.

Abigail's stomach twisted. *Mentoring someone my ass! And with... with TAMMY THE ORGAN PLAYER! What happened to all those nights telling me you wanted to 'wait' and 'do this right' and, and... fucking five years! FIVE YEARS TOGETHER!*

"Abigail?" His voice shrieked. "I... I can explain."

"With Tammy?" Her thoughts were colliding, a constant firework display of sporadic disbelief and pain. "And wouldn't even so much as touch me after groping me two weeks ago? Why even give me..."

Gritting her teeth, she yanked the engagement ring off. With all her might, she gave it a hard-over hand chuck. *At last, that time in little league might pay off for something.* The ring launched with great speed, pinging with a sharp sound off the metal cross above the interlocked couple. Ricocheting with greater speed, it conked off of Pastor Bradley, falling to the floor and rolling right down the drain. *Good! It belongs there!*

"Shit!" He grabbed his face, stumbling away too fast and Tammy landed on her ass on the floor with a great shriek. "My deposit!" He spun and dove for the drain, but his pants intervened. "Shit!" Like any tree, he fell.

"HOW COULD YOU!" Hot tears slid down Abigail's face. "AND WITH THE ORGAN PLAYER! REALLY?"

Who would've thought? An older woman? Is that what he's into? FUCK THIS!

"Hey!" Tammy tried standing but slammed her head on the table she had previously been on. "Dammit, you promised to give me that ring."

"Do you even have a lick of decency?" Abigail's pain shifted into anger. "You red-headed harlot! And you!" She turned on Pastor Bradley, her now ex-fiancé. "Son of a Jezebel! You promised her our ring? The ring you bought me and swore..." She lost the thought, disbelief and heartbreak taking the lead. "What will the congregation think?"

"Don't you dare!" Pastor Bradley rolled to look up at her. "It's your word against mine and Tammy's. The odds are against you if you want to stay in this church."

Abigail gaped. Shaking her head, she wandered out of the room, aimless as she leaned on the hall walls. *Did I hear him right? This unholy son of a bitch is threatening to turn the entire church against me. Can he? Could he? Oh, I'll have to pray on this... What the hell do I do now?*

2

CALL ME DEVIL

Dylan Johnson dried his hair with a hotel towel. Lean, athletic build in a solid six-foot package. His hair black, and eyes just as dark. The tanned skin showed he had frequented the beach plenty of times this year when he didn't haunt the local casinos. He brushed his teeth, fanged like any carnivore-loving fiend. Winking at himself, he rinsed his mouth and strode out into the main room. Tattoos painted his torso, front and back. Layers of black dahlias made a dark background for a devilishly red oni mask on his back, while angels prayed from his upper arms, and tigers crawled across his pecs.

Not a bad start to my Friday.

"Please Dylan. One more time." A naked, tattooed beauty lay tangled in his bed sheets. Her black lipstick and mascara smudged. "I know we just do this to pass the time, but you're a devil in the bed, Dylan."

He snorted, lifting an eyebrow. "That's why they call me Dylan "the Devil" Johnson."

She scoffed, sitting up to stretch her lithe body. "Stop being so smug. It's unbecoming of you."

"Are you refusing to leave unless we go again? I have work to finish. Besides, you need to go home and rest before your night shift later." Dylan twisted his lips, unamused with her delay tactics. "Well?"

Seriously, go home. There's a reason I maintain my privacy. There's no way I'll bring you to my actual room.

She crawled across the bed on all fours, growling, attempting to be sexy. "I'll gobble you up one more time, Dylan. Like a tiger to its prey."

"More like a rabid raccoon," he muttered, just low enough for only him to hear.

She paused. "What did you say?"

"Nothing." He tugged at the towel around his waist, letting it pool around his feet before rushing at her. "Just shut up and fuck me." *If she won't leave, I'll make her want to leave.*

"Yes sir—" He pressed his lips against hers as he climbed onto the bed.

Overpowering her, she rolled back and hugged his neck. The heat of her legs slid across his ribs, and he deepened the kiss. At last, she was on her back, giving him access to rub his hard cock against her lower stomach. Goosebumps washed over her, and she moaned into his mouth. They broke away and he leaned back, letting his hands trail over her shoulders, collarbone, the tender spot between her subtle breasts, until he reached her pussy.

He smirked at her. "Already wet?" he asked, rubbing the opening.

"I was already masturbating while you showered." Biting her lip, she batted her eyes.

She should know better unless she wants me to have the advantage.

"Is that so?" His thumb circled her swollen clit, until she howled, arching her back. "Why yes, you were. I don't know if that's fair." Her knees dug into his muscled ribs as he continued to circle her clit, firmer and faster with each pass. "If I'd known, I could have gotten started while in the shower... I think I ought to punish you."

She gasped. "Not that."

"Oh yea, *that.*" *If you thought I would take it easy after refusing to let me leave without a fuss...*

"W-wait, I could..." She struggled to speak through the waves of pleasure as his slid his other fingers into her wet pussy. "D-Dylan, I... I'll do it."

"Hmm?" He slowed, his dark eyes locking with hers. "You promise what?"

She smirked, failing to stop his hands. "I p-p-promise to swallow."

He stopped, arching a brow. "Funny. If I remember, you told me last week, last night, and I'm pretty sure this morning, that swallowing wasn't your style."

Finally! I'm getting something out of this.

"I did, but I don't think my body can take another round of you pleasuring my pussy, to the level of last night." He let her retreat, his eyes locking on her lips, making his cock throb. "Was it that horrendous?"

"Oh no, it ruined me. Just thinking of you makes me horny." She was back on her hands and knees, the heat of her breath rolling across the tip of his dick. "I just want to return the favor, by taking charge instead."

You lack the same caliber, but I don't know a guy who'd refuse a blow job.

"Are you really going to swallow?" Dylan raised a brow, caressing his knuckles across her spine, flowing down between the hills of her shoulder blades. "I won't play nice if that's the case."

"I'm betting on that."

The heat of her lips flowed over his long, hard shaft. He moaned as her soft, wet tongue wiggled against the underbelly of his dick. His knuckles met the nape of her neck and like a vicious animal, the wrist turned, and he gripped her hair, shoving her further onto his cock. The tip pressed against her throat. His hips rocked, sliding out until the edge of his cap smacked her lips before thrusting forward again.

Her hands crawled across his body, caressing the side and back of his thighs until she squeezed his ass cheeks. He pushed into her deeply once more, and she held him, sucking long, hard, and threatening to swallow his cock whole. Moaning, he closed his eyes, enjoying the heat and tightness of it all.

She did warn she would gobble me up.

The alarm on his watch started to beep. He didn't stop grinding, in and out of her mouth, as he shut it off. *Time to get to work.*

Gripping her hair once more, he let himself relax, soaking in every detail. The way her hard nipples grazed his legs, the hint of nails as she clung to him, even the way the tip of his cock pushed down into— He started moaning more, pressing himself harder into her throat. *Time to swallow, Raccoon Girl.* He glared down, her tongue wiggling, sucking as he started to come. The waves of her mouth and throat tightened around him as she swallowed again and again. Panting, he pulled out. She wiped her lips, the lipstick smudging in a new direction.

Blinking, he looked down to his dick and cursed. "Great, now my dick has a black eye." Rolling away, he shifted into the business-minded casino owner, returning to the bathroom to clean himself up. "Feel free to use this room to wash up before leaving. I'll delay the maid till this afternoon."

She lay on her belly, watching him. "See, I kept my promise."

He laughed. "Yes, you did. You want a cookie or something?"

"Just wish I could spend a Friday or Saturday night with you. The real you, like a proper girlfriend for a change." She frowned. "I suppose I get you on a whim for weekday fun. Are you sure you don't want a relationship?"

He marched back into the room, dressing in a suit and tie. "I'm no one's man."

"Is that so?" She rolled onto her back, stretching her arms out. "What if one of those angels tattooed on your arms spoiled that thought?"

"Then she'd better be worth it," he muttered, buttoning his shirt, then crouching to put on his socks. "By surviving a night of hellfire."

"And I haven't?" She rolled to face him, but he didn't meet her gaze.

"Didn't you just beg to swallow, then attempt a second time?"

She opened her mouth but was at a loss for words.

He chuckled, rising to his feet, and marching to the bathroom. He took a moment to knot his tie and spun back to her. Leaning against the bathroom door frame, he knew he had hurt her pride. "You think you're a tiger, love." His smirk faded. "But you're only a pussy cat—in heat."

"And you're a man whore."

He chuckled. "Never said I wasn't. And besides," grabbing his smartphone off the dresser, "You're a bartender who likes fucking the owner for bragging rights. What makes you better than me?"

The look on her face and her darting eyes told him he was right.

"So, let's not make this more complicated, by making it anything more than one last hoorah." He started for the door, then paused. "It's over, Alexi."

Scoffing, she laughed. "I'll bet my right boob it's not. Not unless you find someone to love or someone willing to keep up with your never-ending libido."

Opening the hotel door, he winked. "Maybe I'll find someone who can do both. Wish me luck."

"Go to hell, Dylan," she barked, cackling.

The door shut loudly in the hallway, and he leaned into the opposite wall. Sighing, he looked at the time. *8:45 AM. Shit, I should've left two hours ago. Why can't that witch of a bartender take no for an answer. Besides, I need to stop drinking so much, or I would've avoided this whole relationship-bullshit drama again.*

His phone buzzed and he answered it. "Yea, yea. I know. I'm late." Rubbing his forehead, he started for the elevator. "Why'd you let me drink so much last night?"

"Where are you?" another male voice asked.

"Upstairs," he drawled.

Laughter erupted. "I knew it! You hooked up with the hot bartender!"

"To be fair, Satch, we hook up often so it's not something to celebrate." He pressed the elevator button and waited. "Are the Morozov's arrangements for their family Gala organized?"

"Yea, boss. It's paid up and the vendors are on schedule. You headed down here to review their work?" He could hear Satch typing on a keyboard. "Or do you want Haley to do it?"

"I'll do it." The elevator opened and he walked in, glad it was empty.

"Do you want either of us to assist?"

"You. I don't want a female around right now." He looked at his reflection, devil horns surfacing in the reflection, but he managed to suppress them, through sheer willpower. "I'm having issues with my shifting today it seems."

"What the hell's going on?" Satch blurted. "You're like the third person this month."

He licked a fang. "Who else? Another devil?"

"My buddy Bif, and a rumor from Gandersville about a Chupacabra."

Dylan paused. "Isn't that where George Worcestershire tried to sell me that ranch?"

"Yea, but he's not a shifter."

"No shit," Dylan scoffed, scanning his keycard, then pressing a button to the top floor. "Is there something in the water?"

"I drank it and nothing's wrong with me." Satch laughed. "We both got laid last night so I can't give you the same advice I told Bif this morning."

"What was that?" Dylan made as face as instant regret hit him.

"Go fuck somebody."

"Sex doesn't solve everything, Satch."

And this is why I can't depend on you. Even when I'm way over my head.

CAN'T HELP FALLING IN LOVE

Abigail's tears wouldn't stop. And she couldn't decide if she cried from a broken heart? Or the pure rage building in her core?

She sat in a back pew, head bowed, praying for relief. There was a lot of foot traffic, but she didn't let that bother her. She wasn't afraid of exposing her puffy red eyes. Normally, Saturdays were a ghost town in the main worship room. Bradley was home, where they lived together, and she couldn't stand the idea of having to see him. Worse, if she went to her family's house, she'd have to endure her brother and the constant pressure of telling him the truth. And she didn't want him in jail for strangling a pastor. Though she had considered this.

Ugh, I keep forgetting they have a deal with the casino in Atlantic City. They meet and load up this morning, but I wanted to be out of the house before Bradley woke up. Of all days to come cry in a pew...

"A-abigail?"

She shot upright at the female voice's owner, alarmed. *No! Why is it someone I know who always sees me at my worst?*

"DeeDee!" In a desperate rush, she wiped her face. "I didn't know you went to the Casino on Saturdays."

"Well, why not? But honestly, I just volunteer to chaperone folks." She slid in and hugged Abigail. "Why are you in a dark corner, crying?"

Busted.

Abigail's gaze landed on the organ. "No. I don't think I can. Just know that Pastor Bradley and I are no longer..." She swallowed, fighting the building tidal wave of tears. "...no longer together."

She refused to look at her friend. Afraid she could see the truth written in her eyes. Still, she couldn't help but wonder: what story he'd tell his colleagues and the congregation tomorrow morning?

Will I even be here? Do I want to attend Sunday service? At least I could...

DeeDee leaned into her vision. "You got plans today?"

"Not anymore," she replied bitterly. *Maybe, never again.*

"Perfect." She grabbed her hand and tugged her out of the church.

"W-wait, DeeDee." They made it through the front doors, the sunlight stinging her eyes. "Where are you taking me?"

"To Atlantic City." She pointed at the bus where a church group and strangers climbed on board. "Come with me, have some fun."

"I..." She looked at herself; Baggy sweatpants and oversized shirts were her only go-to attire since walking in on Pastor Bradley and Tammy. "I can't go like this."

I feel like a mobile couch potato who forgot her chips at home!

"Of course, you can." Bracing a hand on the bus door to keep it from closing, Abigail listened as Deidre continued her mischievous plan. "Sweats are great for a long bus ride. We'll go shopping once we're there."

She's going to shove me on this bus!

Abigail's face heated, the heel of DeeDee's hands shoved into her back. "With what money!"

I only have a small purse, a phone, and my license! Is she mad?

"My money if I have to." She put her elbow into the small of Abigail's back, earning a yelp. "I'm buying. So, walk up those steps and grab us a seat, would ya?"

DeeDee! You won't give up and I am too tired to...

Back aching, Abigail folded. She let go and went fumbling forward with DeeDee toppling onto her. The bus driver looked down his steps at them, completely baffled by their actions. Righting themselves, they laughed and gave him a nod as they climbed on board. The two of them ignored the glares from the other passengers.

"You're so embarrassing," Abigail hissed, smirking as they sat in the first open side.

"I know, but I got a laugh and smile from you. That's all that matters." DeeDee beamed, elbowing her in the ribs as she chuckled. "You'll see. This is a lot of fun."

The bus door slammed shut, the air brake hissing as it released. Then the vehicle surged forward. Abigail's stomach knotted, her smile starting to fade. She was surrounded by unfamiliar faces, minus her friend's. *At least if I embarrass myself, none of them will tattle to the pastor.* As she took them all in, her brow furrowed, and she looked back at DeeDee.

"Do any of these people even go to our church?" she whispered.

She shrugged. "Nope. I only see them on Saturday bus rides."

"Uh, but I thought you had to be a member to buy a ticket?" Abigail sunk into her seat, fiddling with the pendant on her necklace.

At least I can wear this again. It might bring me some luck.

"They never said you had to attend to be considered a church member." DeeDee watched with intrigue as Abigail rolled the sunstone between her fingers. "What is that?"

"Oh, this?" She let it dangle, the edges of the gemstone translucent while the center burst red like a droplet of blood caught in crystal. "Just an old family heirloom."

"It's gorgeous. I've never seen you wear it before."

"Well, Bradley..." She choked and forced the words out. "My ex didn't like me wearing it. Said it was creepy. It didn't help that my great granny called it the Devil's Stone. Not exactly appropriate for a pastor's wife... to... never mind. That doesn't matter anymore."

If I ever see Tammy again, I swear...

DeeDee snorted. "Something tells me I'll need you really drunk to learn the full story."

"I might not tell you even if I get shitfaced." Abigail dropped the necklace and shifted her gaze to the bus window.

"Well, time for rollcall and see who's coming back and who's staying." DeeDee paused and spun back. "In fact, do you want to stay?"

Abigail shrugged, refusing to meet her gaze. Tears wavered on the edge of her eyelids.

Maybe I should stay. Besides, I'm so pissed at him. I just know I wouldn't be able to keep my mouth shut the moment he looked over at me, Tammy, or even the damn organ itself. My mother played on that organ before that harlot defiled it and my fiancé. Now I look at it and all I see is those two fucking, all over again.

It wasn't long before the exhaustion from crying and the white noise of a three-hour drive had lulled her to sleep. Only waking as the heat of DeeDee's hand shook her shoulder, her thoughts still stinging in her chest. *Did I blink away the trip, I just got on the bus, didn't I?*

DeeDee pointed to Abigail's chin, giving her a sympathetic expression. Alarmed, she wiped the line of drool from her face. *I didn't sleep at all last night. Of all the places to completely pass out.* Abigail vacated the bus, standing before the entrance to the *Saint's Hotel and Casino.* With a rumble, the bus rode away, revealing a grandiose fountain, large and obscuring whatever view from the other side of the massive pool.

She spun back to the doors, heart racing, and a smile forming on her lips. *Why not forget about it all; live my life like I used to when I did pub crawls and club hops. I'm a free woman and I'm officially on the rebound! First, let's get out of these sweats and into something cute.*

"You said you were buying?" She lifted an eyebrow at DeeDee.

Grinning, she hooked her arm in Abigail's and led her into the lobby. "Yes, ma'am. And I know exactly what you need."

They traversed the crowds, bypassing the casino entrance to a row of novelty shops. Before she could catch the name on the sign, DeeDee had her in a small room, crowded with tuxedos, suits, and cocktail dresses.

DeeDee weaved them through the towers of hangers, before settling on a long skirted black velvet cocktail dress. "Now give me a chance," she announced, thrusting the dress into Abigail's hands. "I know you normally wear brighter colors, but this is better suited at mourning the death of your engagement."

I'm too plump to pull that dress off. Even if I love the gold embroidery and ribbons that lace-up the back.

Abigail snorted. "Black cocktail dress. What ball am I attending?" She returned it to the rack and grabbed a softer, pink-colored dress, a design she felt more comfortable wearing. "I don't want to give the wrong impression of others assuming I have money. If I'm dancing and drinking, I want to feel at home. Be myself ... again."

"Aww, live a little." DeeDee pouted, slumping her shoulders in defeat. "Fine. I'll get you that one if you at least wear those cute sandals with it."

"Do they have size 9?" Abigail cringed, feeling like she had hobbit feet.

"Sure do!" interjected the sales associate. She eyed Abigail and declared her assumption. "Aww, first night out after having the baby."

The woman paled under Abigail's stare, but DeeDee chimed in, coming between them. "Bad breakup. You know how it is, the bigger and baggier the clothes, the better."

Did she just mistake me for freshly pregnant? Looking down, Abigail puffed out her cheeks. *Yeah, ok. This outfit isn't flattering and makes me look ten times fatter.*

"Oh." Her voice came out weak and she said, "Sorry, with the sweats on... look, I can give you an additional fifteen percent off your entire purchase. If you need anything at all, just ask. And happy hunting tonight, ladies!"

Looking at the shoes and pink dress, Abigail sucked on the inside of her cheek. "Fine. If it gets me out of these sweats and everyone thinking I'm a new mom, it's worth the discount."

I think I'm going to hit the slots first! And maybe, if I'm feeling frisky, find myself a one-night stand!

It didn't take long to dress and with DeeDee's help, her hair was woven into a simple updo.

DeeDee handed her some chips and the two headed for the casino floor. The neon lights gave the place a mixture of other-worldly meets adult arcade vibe. Combined with the *cha-ching*'s of slots and shouts from the Blackjack table, it added fuel to her rising adrenaline rush. The first slot machine she met, she placed a chip in, pulled the lever and... *CLUNK-CLUNK-CLUNK... a complete bust.*

"Abby, don't stop after one try." DeeDee nudged her. "Second chances for the win, right?"

Another chip in the slot. The cranking of the lever and the rollers spun, blurring the images written on them. Again, they stopped, one after another. And again, bust. Abigail's temper rose and she repeated this until she'd burnt through every chip. NOTHING.

I can't win at love, life, or luck. This is shitty. Gripping the charm, she scoffed at it. *Some lucky charm you make.*

"I need a drink." DeeDee furrowed her brow and walked toward a dark corner near blue neon accents, and images of flames and clouds. "DeeDee, I think I'm cursed."

"Oh, c'mon. You can't really believe that?" They grabbed a pair of empty stools and waited for the bartender to finish with her current customers. "Exactly, what happened between you and Bradley?"

And there it is. Abigail scowled, ignoring the question. *I've got to avoid answering at all costs.*

The bartender spun around, the girl tattooed, tall, and skinny, unlike herself. Abigail was curvy and petite, but she didn't feel pretty lately. Bradley had stopped complimenting her weeks ago. Her confidence had left her long ago, being with someone for five years does that to a person.

I bet she could catch any guy in this joint. What I wouldn't give for a body like that. I wouldn't have to try to find a man, they'd line up out the door.

DeeDee leaned into Abigail's ear and said, "Is it me or does her smoky eyeshadow look a little heavy?"

A smirk lifted the corner of her mouth. "She looks like a raccoon," she muttered low, so the approaching bartender couldn't overhear.

Ok, I suppose with makeup like that, she'd come off as one-night stand material. Maybe I should go edgy too?

"Welcome to Purgatory, our special tonight is two for one Dead End Margaritas and Second Life Cocktails."

"Give me both," Abigail blurted without hesitation. *I've hit a dead end and need a second life really bad.*

"Those guys are staring at us." DeeDee elbowed Abigail and she grimaced. "What kind of response is that?"

"They're too handsome for like a plain girl like me." The first drink slid to her, and she started gulping it down. *If I'm going to have any chance at a rebound, I'll have to settle with a less dangerous, smaller fry. Those look like the sort of men with deep pockets and...*

"I think they're interested Abigail." DeeDee smirked, raising her brow high. "The one pointed over here. There's no one else at the bar but us."

"Yea right." The bartender returned, pushing the other drink toward her. "How much do we owe you?"

Poor DeeDee, she's blown a lot of money on me. I don't know how much these damn drinks cost.

The bartender looked Abigail over before nodding her head toward the handsome men still staring at them. "Dylan's buying all your drinks tonight. You might just get lucky and find yourself sleeping with the Devil tonight. I'm jealous. He's never bought me a drink."

Abigail choked on her margarita, locking eyes with the man who raised a drink in acknowledgment. Her eyes widened as she gripped her pendant. His friend covered his face in sheer embarrassment. *Oh, I feel you, buddy. Your friend is a bit much for me, drunk or sober. Duly noted: The Devil just bought my drinks and wants to sleep with me. Time to enjoy free drinks but avoid that man in the pin-striped suit at all costs. What ridiculous odds I have when it comes to bad luck.*

4

DEVIL'S PLAYGROUND

Dylan pulled on his overcoat, glad to leave his top floor office. As he pushed through his office door, Satch leaned on the counter talking to his secretary, Yvette. Arching one eyebrow, he listened a moment before clearing his throat, bringing them to attention. The Morozov family had invested in the casino and hotel from the beginning, so it was the least he could do when he hired their youngest daughter.

"You two play a dangerous game," he chuckled. "None of my business. Are you joining me tonight, Satch?"

"I don't understand why you play the roulette table every night, just to prove your luck." Satch winked at Yvette, then followed Dylan down the hallway. "You don't even take the chips. It's a waste."

"If you missed the memo, I'm the COO for the whole place. Why do I need to take my own money?" Snorting, he waited for the elevator doors to close. "Seriously, flirting and dating a Morozov girl is dangerous. They'll kill you over it. In fact, I'm convinced they started the Russian mafia when they migrated north from the Himalayan Mountains. You don't fuck with Yetis."

"Do I look scared?" Satch made a suave face.

"No." Dylan straightened his tie in the reflection of the metal doors. Then made eye contact with Satch. "You look like an idiot."

"You're cruel to your PA's, Boss Man."

"That's what you think." The doors opened to a cacophony of music and slot machines. "I never grow tired of this."

"Hey, hey!" Satch elbowed him, nodding at two women near the slots. "That's a regular, but the girl in the sundress, she's new. Whatcha think?"

"And what makes you think I'm looking for new prospects?" He then locked eyes with the roulette table tenant, and they frowned noticing his smirk. "I've got luck to play with."

Satch stepped into his view, unamused. "No, really dude. Tell me what you see. It's killing me. I can't peg your type, and I'm curious. You're settling for less than what you deserve. I've never seen you be with a girl beyond a quickie then you're out."

Shit, has he figured me out so easily? Damn it, I hired him for his insightful talent, but this is backfiring in unexpected ways.

Dylan scowled. "I can say the same. Does Yvette know you're flirting with every vagina at the bar last night."

"Far as I know, she's using me to get back at her Daddy or Big Bro for whatever reason." He rolled his eyes. "Humor me tonight."

I was thinking the same thing... so he's just an opportunist.

Huffing, Dylan spun back to the girls at the slots, observing as the temper flared on the new girl. *Bust after bust. I need to check the odds on that machine, shit.* The regular he recognized as one of the church volunteers from Philadelphia. He was terrible with names, but his assistants kept track of the details.

His glare shifted back to the other girl, and he blinked. She wore a scowl, not a face he preferred his customers to have when they came here to unwind for the weekend. She was a natural beauty, a rare sight in a casino where most tended to overdress in cocktail dresses and pressed suits. Her minimalistic makeup and pink sundress were a warm contrast to her cool brown skin. The curves of her body were inviting.

If she's sassy, fiery, or even the slightest bit bossy... He spun back to the roulette table, marching toward it with dread weighing down on him. *Everything about her is my type. But I'm not in the place to settle down with someone. Commitment is the last thing I want, and that's the kind of girl you date long term, hell, even put a ring on. My life is managing this place and having the flexibility to sleep with any stranger I want. I love my life! I think I do? Who the hell am I kidding? I'm fucking lonely...*

"Hey!" Satch caught up, baffled. "You didn't tell me."

"I'm not shallow like you Satch. Everyone woman is beautiful in their own way. So yes, she's pretty if that's what you wondered."

"Ok. Mr. Philosophical. You got a point." He snatched two cocktails from a passing tray. "But would you take her upstairs if *she* offered?"

"I don't sleep with women like that."

"Like what?" Glowered Satch, denying Dylan's reach for one of the drinks.

"The kind you take back home to mom and marry." He claimed his drink and emptied it, then abandoned it on a side table with another cluster of empty glasses. "What kind of monster do you take me for? I'm not interested in breaking hearts."

"I'm betting hers is already broken and she's on the rebound. Do her a favor by having her sleeping with someone of your reputation." Satch sipped his drink, knowing full-well Dylan was fighting the tide of temptation.

Rebound. That doesn't make this ok to take advantage.

"Is that so?" When they reached the roulette table, he pulled a stack of chips from his inner coat pocket, placing them on red nineteen.

"Again," added the dealer.

Where's he going with this?

Dylan winked at him, leaning back to watch the other suitors place bets. "If you're implying that I need to be her rebound, forget it."

"Oh, so we are continuing this discussion, are we?" Satch finished his drink, a dangerous glint in his eye.

"What are the chances you pegged her? So what if she's on the rebound? Or a girl's night out? Maybe her cat died?" Dylan snorted, and the roulette wheel spun to life. "You're assuming too much."

Satch leaned back into the table, watching the commotion on the floor. "Nope. I'm telling you. The look in her eyes ... she's on a rebound. Maybe undecided on how far she's willing to go. She's a long way from Philly and a first timer to the casino. I bet her friend dragged her here against her will."

There it is. That thing he does where he picks apart the target on a particular topic as if he knows it by pure instinct. Intuition of a Sasquatch, I suppose. This isn't a board meeting, so it's him, being him.

A smirk formed on Dylan's face. "You got proof?"

"Oh yea." The roulette wheel slowed, the ball teasing along a set of numbers. "That dress is from our shop. And she lost hard at the slots, now heading for Purgatory. She wants to get shit faced first, but I doubt she has the money. That's why her friend has that concerned look. In fact, the downstairs sales associate was in tears because she called a girl fat or preggers or something; I bet it was these two. I had to clear a discount she offered them."

"We sell that dress?" The ball landed in black twenty. He leaned in, wide-eyed. "I lost."

My luck never fails me unless...

"You lost," echoed the dealer, his eyes widened. "That's a first. Again?"

Dylan frowned. "No, it seems my luck has a new game in mind."

Satch, this is your fault. You knew it before I did. Fuck. Sasquatch intuition is a beast.

Silent and stoic, Dylan left the roulette table and headed for the bar, his focus recalling the woman's beauty and sadness. *Yes. A broken look of desperation, of wanting to forget. The bar's a horrible idea. What's her friend thinking? Or was this her idea?*

He wound through the bustling casino with practiced skill, Satch following. They entered the dark bar like two predators, the blue neon casting ambiguous shadows. Satch aimed for the empty seats near the girls who were now talking to the bartender, but Dylan dragged him to the opposite end. He forced him to sit, and he joined him.

The bartender turned and cracked a wide smile.

Shit, I forgot Racoon Girl was working tonight.

Satch waved her over. "Hey! Put her drinks on Dylan's tab. Tell her he's buying."

She turned to Dylan, and he shrugged. "Sure, why not."

"Ok, and here's some dirty martinis. The new waitress couldn't handle a full load." She slid them over but didn't let go of Dylan's drink. "If she doesn't pan out, you know my number."

With that, she left, and Dylan covered his face. "How do I get myself into these situations?"

"The Devil's luck." Satch waved at the girls, excited like a teenage boy. "Sounds like you and Alexi had fun last night... or was that this morning? Both, hey-hey!"

"Stop it. And sit down. You look like an amateur wingman in that pin-striped suit." Dylan laughed into his hand. "In fact, I wouldn't be shocked if she avoids you—no us, after buying her drinks. If she's smart enough, she'll ghost us both when she sees an opening."

"Well, you're the one that should hook up with her. Yvette's getting jealous lately." At last, Satch settled into his seat. "Are you?"

"Am I what?" drawled Dylan, nursing his drink as he stole a glance at the curly haired beauty. *Dammit, she caught me staring.*

"Interested in a bet?"

Dylan raised an eyebrow at Satch's words. "What kind of bet?"

"That she won't hook up with you."

Dylan shook his head, baffled. "But you insisted I hook up with her. What gives?"

"Right. I was aiming to get you interested into someone new, but..." He snorted. "Look. See how fast she's downing those drinks? You'll be lucky if she says two coherent words to you. I think I underestimated how broken-hearted she is and like you said, that's not your strong suit."

"Not my strong suit." Dylan echoed. "What makes you say that?"

Satch met Dylan's glare with smug expression. "You're too much of a hard-ass to be able to handle a girl that fragile."

Dylan set his drink down and watched the two girls talk. Their conversation turned serious, and her friend frowned, hugging her. Whatever happened, she'd finally told her friend the truth. Her eyes wandered to Satch, her brow lowering as she sucked her drink through a straw. Her friend said something and motioned their way. She shook her hands and locked eyes with him. Chills rolled over him, something electrifying and triggering that Devil's Luck high the roulette table had denied him.

I can't remember the last time I felt this excited about meeting a girl's gaze. So that's where my luck went. I mean, it's just for tonight, right? What do I have to lose?

"Fine. I accept your bet. What do you want if you win?" Dylan shifted, unamused at Satch's toothy grin.

"Alexi's number."

He laughed. "Ha. Deal. And now, we wait."

"Wait? For what?" Satch sipped his drink. "For her to be alone? How old school are you playing this?"

He gave a stern glance to Satch. "I'm waiting for my annoying PA to leave so I can actually make a move. You've already botched the approach."

Satch choked on his drink. "Fine." He cleared his throat. "If you really think you can succeed without your best wingman, then go, Boss Man."

With that, Satch walked away. Messing with his phone.

[Satch: I want to know every detail in the morning. You owe me that much!]

[Dylan: Don't you have to go get your buddy Bif out of trouble?]

[Satch: He's a big guy. I doubt mister redneck bigfoot needs my help.]

Dylan finally relaxed. He watched the two women, then checked his watch. *The church bus would load in the next hour.* Alexi circled back, continuing to fuel him and the broken-heart girl with drinks.

"Do you want her name?" she teased.

He glimpsed at the girl as she played with the straw on her margarita. "You trying to help me get laid with someone other than you, Alexi? I don't know how I feel about that."

"Abigail. Or was it, Abby?" She bit her dark lipstick.

"I imagine both." He sucked on his cheek. "So, tell me, what makes you so invested in my interest."

She smirked. "If anyone here tonight qualified as angel status, you may have found it, Mr. Devil."

"Oh?" Again, they locked eyes and Abby shot her eyes downward, brow furrowing. "I suppose telling her she has nice shoes; let's fuck would work as well as it did on you."

Alexi cackled, grabbing up a rag and starting to wipe down the bar top. "You got my number."

"I do, and if this goes in the right direction, Satch will also have your number." He hid his smirk behind the martini glass as he sipped it.

"Don't you dare." Dread filled her face.

Time dragged by and this time when Dylan glanced back to the girl, she was alone.

Her friend gone.

Finally. I got to give it to Satch; he knew I'd wait. He peered at his watch and paled. *When the hell did it hit closing time? Shit! Her bus left already!* Panic washed over him. Looking back to her she was ... gone. He jerked to his feet, glancing around the bar. *Where the hell did she go? Shit, she ghosted! She couldn't have gone far.*

"You ok, Dylan?" The bartender started grabbing the empty martini glasses. "If you're looking for the girl, she muttered something about church?"

"Dammit, my luck is failing me tonight." He bolted from his seat.

"Don't give that sasquatch my number!" Alexi crossed her arms.

Since when did I have bad luck and bad timing? What the hell is wrong with me tonight?

5

LUCKY

*T*he man in the pin-striped suit left early, but his friend still lingered.

Abigail ordered another round of margaritas and narrowed her eyes at him. He had dark hair and sharp features. This was the kind of man she'd seen in cologne advertisements in a doctor's lobby, wondering whether they truly existed. *Yes, they do.* She laughed, sucking on the straw, humming to herself.

Any girl would feel like a queen sleeping with a guy like that. But hot guys are jerks. Yet… Shit. I need dick.

DeeDee shook her shoulder. "Abby, it's time to go."

"I'm staying," she slurred. "Go on without me." *I haven't found dick yet, but I can't tell you that!*

DeeDee sighed. "Abigail, I can't wait for you," she said, turning away. "Call me if you need a ride home. I'll pick you up or I'll get you a Guber."

"Home is a shit show." She shoved the empty glass away and slid the other drink to her. "I live with him, DeeDee. He told me to save it for marriage, but he gave himself to Tammy instead. You know who that bitch reminds me of? Meredith. From *The Office*. What. The. Fuck. I'm no virgin and neither was he..."

Besides, I can't hunt for a rebound with you still here. You're every bit as daring, if not more. I can't do this with a witness. Go! Leave! This is a risk I'm willing to take if it means forgetting that whole scene in the Baptism room!

"It's ok. You can stay with me when you decide to come home to Philly. I have a couch that will do." Deidre gave her a hug. "Are you sure you want to stay here all night? Alone?"

Abigail sighed. "Yeah. This is my last drink. I'm buzzed but not belligerent. Though I wish I were and could stop the heartache from swelling in my chest. I just need a break from Philly for a while. Come back for me tomorrow if I haven't called."

"Ok. But here, just in case." She slipped a twenty-dollar bill into Abigail's purse. "Remember, the buffet is free. So are the mimosas. Take it easy, girlie." With that, she left.

The bartender came over. "Hey, sweetheart," she said. "I closed your tab; we're closing for the night, but the casino runs all night. Breakfast starts at seven if you're in for the long haul."

"Aww." She pouted, abandoning her last margarita before slurring, "But I'm not drunk enough to forget the organ-play-er-*fucking* pastor."

The bartender laughed. "I don't know what happened but promise to share your story with me sometime."

Sighing, Abigail pulled away and stumbled into the buzz of bodies on the casino floor. Her head swam as thoughts collided from shouts and dings of the slots. The glow of signs featuring saints, angels, and devils seemed to charge at her.

What the hell am I doing? Am I really going this far? No, no...

She searched the room, anxiety tightening her chest. *I need fresh air. No, I need to go home. Is the bus still here? Hell. I'm not that one-night stand kind of girl anymore.*

At last, she caught sight of the lobby. She'd come through it, to reach the casino, that much she remembered. Shoving through scores of people, she began singing to herself, focusing on the lyrics to calm herself. With the fog of alcohol, she couldn't tell if she lipped them or sang them out loud. A few double takes and looks from people made it clear she sang it aloud and her choice of music slammed several patrons with nostalgic smirks.

I don't care if they can hear me. Keep singing, keep your mind off the situation.

The doors opened and she faced the fountain, glowing and shifting colors against the stark black night. She mumbled to herself; the singing continuing as she stared in awe. Inhaling deeply for a moment, she closed her eyes. It was quiet and the song kept playing in her mind, stopping the thoughts, and letting her anxiety fall away.

Her phone buzzed: a text message. Several actually.

[DeeDee: We had to leave, love. Please stay safe and call me when you're ready to return to Philly. XOXO DeeDee]

SHIT! The bus! It's too late to change my mind. I'm stuck. Calling her now would make her feel bad. What was I thinking? I can't do this, I can't go home, and I can't even go to church.

She started to cry. Digging in her tiny purse, she cursed under her breath. All she had was her identification and her phone... *oh, and twenty bucks.* Her tears felt heavy, but she kept on singing *Lucky*, hoping Britney Spears would save her from this emotional breakdown.

Her phone started ringing; the screen read: *Bradley.*

Panic jolted her. She threw her phone hard and fast. *Get out of my life already!*

The bellhop blinked and whistled. "I've never seen anyone throw that good. And it's the first time someone's hit the fountain from the front door."

Panic shifted into rage. *How the hell am I getting home! I haven't remembered a phone number since before cell phones were affordable!* She tossed her purse, pissed at overthrowing the phone into the fountain.

Splash!

Gasping, she covered her mouth and stumbled backward. *Damn little league! No-no-no-no! What did I just do!* She clung to the song once more, aiming to calm herself.

A hand tapped her shoulder and she spun, singing the main chorus.

The handsome stranger furrowed his brow. "Lonely heart? Are you singing?"

Tears fell, and she lost her voice, her singing falling apart. *The other man from the bar found me. Dammit. Do I have to sleep with someone to get out of this?*

"Calm down." He examined the fountain a minute before his gaze returned to her. "D-did you just throw your stuff in my fountain?"

"Y-yes," she wailed. "I'm sorry, I'm drunk." *Just go all in, Abby. Play the rebound card like you did at the clubs in college.*

"I see." He gave her a pitiful expression. "You're quite the mess; we can't have that. You should be enjoying yourself. I imagine you came here to escape..."

"He fucked the organ player." His eyes widened, and she covered her mouth. *Why the hell did I say that!*

"Ok. Not sure if I've ever seen a sexy organ player, but maybe he did you a favor?" The man waved the bellhop over. "Timmy, add a note to the maintenance log. Tell them to bring me a box of any contents found in the fountain by tomorrow morning."

Oh shit. Is this guy the manager? How embarrassing! I can't handle much more of this...

"To your room directly?" His eyes shifted to Abigail, covering her face. "She's got an arm, Boss. She tossed her phone from there."

"And her purse. Yes, she should have pitched for a Major League Baseball team. Perhaps, the Yankees wouldn't have lost their last game."

"Right?"

Abigail glared at them, unamused as she wiped the running mascara and tears from her face.

"Does she need an escort to her room?" added the bellhop.

"I don't hav—" Dylan hugged her into him, muffling her in the warmth of his chest. *Wait, do I know this man? Why is he hugging me? Oh my, he smells nice. Cologne magazine looks and smell! He's the complete package!*

"Don't worry." He rubbed her back, and she wiggled in his embrace. "I got her. She's pretty upset."

The bellhop strode through the automatic doors, and Dylan released her. Her crying had ceased, but her eyes shifted into anger. Temper rising, she searched for words, but the haze of alcohol stilled her. Flashes from the bar made her realize—*he waited all night to get me alone.*

She shoved him back, her feet clumsy, missing the curb.

"SHIT!" Yelping, she tensed as she fell backward.

His arms wrapped around her. She froze as he pressed her into his chest, against his soft cotton shirt and pricey cologne. And the way his arms shielded her, so strong and gentle, she couldn't help but lean into him.

He sighed.

I give up.

"I don't know who you are, but something tells me you're in quite the predicament." She nodded against him. "Were you supposed to be on that bus back to Philly?" Another shake of her head as she confessed in silent defeat. "All right. Now, if you're calm, I'd like to have your name in exchange for mine."

Sniffling, she pulled out of his arms. "Abigail Montgomery."

"May I call you Abby?" She met his eyes; the dark pools were mesmerizing, and the horns peeking from his forehead seemed so *realistic*. "I'm Dylan Johnson, the COO for the Saint's Hotel and Casino."

"Dylan, The Devil," she mumbled, echoing the bartender's words as she lifted her fingers to touch a horn.

His eyes widened, cupping her hand, and slid across her fingers until he reached the horn. Dylan searched the air and spun around. There, he narrowed his eyes at his reflection on the glass walls and swallowed. Reaching for Abigail's hand, he held it tight, leading her back into the bustling casino. Before she could gauge where he was leading her, they were in an elevator.

He scanned a card and it ascended.

Where is he taking me?

Curious, she watched him peer into the metal doors, flicking a finger at a horn. "Shit. What the hell triggered this to appear again?"

"The bartender." Her tongue let loose, still aimed to spite her efforts in following her plan to play the rebound card. She cursed the margaritas. "She said if I was lucky, I'd get to sleep with the devil himself. She was talking about you, wasn't she?"

I get it. This is on par. I'm next on your menu. That's ok, I need a place to stay the night, I did say I needed dick, and this counts as an epic rebound, right? And maybe...

He palmed his face, turning to her. "Look, about that..."

The elevator doors opened, and she marched out with a new sense of resolve. "Let's get this over with. I suppose I've got nothing else to lose. Not like I'm a virgin or anything."

"Abby." He caught up to her, and she paused.

This isn't a hotel room. Holy cow.

The entire floor was like walking into a mansion. In one corner, a mini gym overlooked the beach, the leather couches were arranged before a large screen television, even a kitchen that could hold the entire staff from her local Applebee's, and a hallway hinted there would be far more to see.

"I can get you a room, it's on me." He snorted as the elevator closed behind them. "And no, there's no need to offer me anything. I don't trade sexual favors for free lodging. I might be loose, but I'm not a douchebag." He walked past her, aiming for the hallway. "Make yourself at home."

He disappeared down the corridor, the rise of her anxiety prompting her to follow. "Wait!" *He can't leave me here alone in this, this monstrous penthouse!*

Dylan turned to meet her panicked face. "Yes? You want a room?"

"I..." Swallowing, her face flushed. *I can't believe I'm about to say this. And to a complete stranger, but the idea of it.* "I don't want to be alone."

A smile bloomed on his face. "Then follow me to the master bedroom. You can have my bed tonight. Without me in it, of course." He motioned for her to take the lead. "Last door. The rest is an office I use when I don't want to go downstairs or as a backup security room for monitoring the casino. Sorry. There's no spare bedroom in this place."

"It's fine. Just my luck, not your fault." Passing through the open door, she slowed and spun.

The bed was massive, matching the chest and elegant dresser filling the walls and the leather loveseat opposite the headboard. Turning back to Dylan, he tossed his coat and shirt to the floor. Her breath caught. He was stacked, and the array of tattoos gave her an excuse to admire his muscles and broad build. Oriental dragons and koi sleeved his arms and wrists. He turned his back to her, and she gasped once more. A devilish face met her gaze.

He froze, realizing what she saw, then chuckled. "It doesn't bite." He smirked, enjoying her curiosity. "Want to touch it?"

"It's terrifying and beautiful." Abigail stepped closer, admiring the red and yellow oni mask that stretched his entire backside. Her fingers traced the mask's tears, while her eyes tracked the hints of a serpentine dragon. "Did it hurt?"

"Less than a broken heart." They locked eyes for a moment, but he walked into the bathroom, then leaned into the vanity.

What's that look for? "The horns, they match," she added, intrigued by the emotions he sparked deep inside her.

They locked gazes through the mirror. "The horns... I suppose I should explain them, but it's not what you would expect. I consider myself a modern version of the New Jersey Devil. A shifter, but it doesn't normally happen unless I wanted to ... impress you."

I don't know what the hell he's talking about, but...

"The tattoo. Does that represent you?" He tilted his head as if unsure how to reply. "It's sad, like your eyes."

Dylan's head slumped in defeat. "Yea, it's how I perceive myself. A devil with no hope."

Is it wrong, wanting to hug him? Feel those arms around me one more time?

She walked into the bathroom, lost in the size of his shower. "Oh my..." Kicking off the sandals, she began removing her sundress. "Now, I want a shower."

Damn this unfiltered sense of self. Why can't I be this confident all the time? Or is it clear he has no intention of taking advantage, that I feel this way? And is it wrong to secretly hope he would?

6

BE YOUR MAN

Dylan watched Abigail through the vanity mirror like a
predator lurking in the grass. He bit his lip, his canines a
little bigger than before, his horns continuing to grow. If
he ever felt like the devil, it was in this moment. The girl hadn't
planned on hooking up with him, but still, the cute cherry print
cotton panties and matching bra tickled his fancy.

She reached behind her back and fumbled to unhook her bra.

"You do realize I'm still in here, right?" From this angle,
Dylan couldn't see her face, but the contours of her soft, curvy
body stirred his arousal, fueling his dark desires. "Or are you so
drunk you don't care?"

Dammit, is she trying to seduce me or put me in the friend zone?

"You're not my first one-night stand," she blurted, finally
unlatching the bra, and sliding it off her arms. "I used to live
that wild life of clubbing and hooking up in the bathroom or
back alley."

He laughed, catching a glimpse of side boob and an erect nipple before her arm obscured the view. "And here I thought you were a church woman."

"I am. Or was. Well ... until I caught him cheating." She paused, her thumbs hooking the top of her panties. "I can't go back. Not when I can run into Tammy. I need to find another church?"

She couldn't have been... what are the chances? I wonder...

He waited as she paused from shedding her last stitch of clothes, hungry to see all of her. "I've got to ask. Why the hell sent you to my casino, to lose yourself to margaritas for an entire night?"

She glanced over her shoulder, locking eyes with his reflection. "Would you believe me if I said I was once engaged to a pastor?"

Dylan lifted his brow. "You're very pretty. So that isn't a far stretch."

"Not pretty enough." She fussed and slid her panties off.

When was the last time I got a chance to sleep with a girl like her? Shit, was it the last actual relationship? She's the kind of girl you take back to mom all right, even if she's drunk and unfiltered. No, that's not true. This whole time she's been distraught but she's not slurring.

"So what happened? I take it the engagement is null and void." He leaned into the vanity, watching as she bent down, stepping out of her panties. "For a girl comfortable in her birthday suit, why would he leave you?"

"That's the alcohol." She didn't turn around, her face hidden once more as she stood, holding her arms.

Good thing she's not looking this way, I'm getting hard just taking her body in with my eyes.

"Says the girl who once hooked up in back alleys and has the pitching arm fit for the Boston Red Sox."

That march of confidence, but her eyes and words just don't match it. There's a story behind that pretty face, and she has my full attention. I want to know more. What about her makes my body want to shift, though?

She stepped into the large shower, standing before a cluster of showerheads and knobs. "Well, apparently Tammy was prettier."

"Ah, so that's what happened." He wrenched his lips, watching as she twisted knobs, failing to turn on the shower. "How did you find out?"

At least she's willing to answer my questions. What an ass though. Really? The organ player? Over this gorgeous, sassy, mulatto girl? Did he lose his nerve to get married?

Dylan's eyes took her in; the curves of her hips and ass made his erection throb.

Sorry, Raccoon Girl, it seems I prefer my girls plump and saucy. I'm in so much trouble with someone like Abby. Dammit, but will a pastor's ex-fiancée allow me near her with fangs and horns fit for the devil himself. At this rate, my wings and tail will burst out too. And that hasn't happened since college when I got wasted at the Bridgewater Triangle.

She put her hands on her hips, and Dylan bit his lip again. "I walked in on them, fucking in the baptism room."

"Ouch." He stepped from the vanity and walked up behind her. *Would she let me... could we...?*

"How does this fucking fancy shower even work?"

Temptation won out. He slipped his arms through the triangular gaps bracketing Abby. Elbows clamped down, only pushing his muscular arms against her hips as they slid forward and pulled on the center knob. Water sputtered over them, and she yelped. He didn't flinch as the first burst of cold soon warmed. Bracing his palms on the gray and white marble tiles, he started kissing her neck, then her shoulder, inhaling her sweet perfume. She arched into him. Head tilting her wet body against his torso, their bodies hot and wet. His hard cock pushed against her, rubbing against the top of her hip with nothing but a thin layer of fabric between them.

"I want the big one," she breathed.

Pausing, he blinked as his brow furrowed. "What?"

"That shower head up there," she pointed, "if we're gonna fuck in the shower, I want the big one."

Shit, she's drunker than I thought. I can't go through with this.

Puffing out his cheeks, Dylan obliged. He pulled the top knob, and a warm waterfall rained over them. She laughed, a smile gracing her face at last, making her eyes sparkle. He caught his breath and pulled away, leaving her alone in the shower. Abandoning his drenched pants on the floor beside her own clothes, he attempted to dry his hair with a towel, cursing as the fabric snagged on the horns.

"Wait." Her voice made him pause, his back still turned to her. "I thought we were about to have awesome shower sex."

He scoffed. "I can't tell if you're too drunk to regret this later or not. So, forget it. Enjoy the shower."

Agitated, he walked out of the bathroom and began pacing. A few times, he eyed the leather chair, wondering if he'd have time to jack off. His erection throbbed as his mind shifted the thought, imagining himself sitting there, watching her masturbate on the bed with...

"Son of a bitch." He covered his face. "This is your fault Satch. What a fucking mess."

He went to the bedroom door. The sound of something crashing in the bathroom made him pause. Then a whimper made him charge for the open bathroom door. Inhaling deep, a moan from her made him panic, and he forced himself to return there.

Inside the shower, Abigail was sitting on the marble bench, her head and back pressed up against the glass as steam filled the room.

"Hey, you ok?" he asked, stopping on the step down. She didn't respond. "Are you getting sick on me?"

Her shoulders slumped, and she frowned. His eyes flowed from her shoulder, down a slender arm until they reached where her fingers touched her pussy. *You've got to be fucking kidding me, what kind of luck...* Dylan swallowed, paling as a revelation came to him. *The Devil's luck.* Abigail looked away, uncaring and miserable as she attempted to continue playing with herself.

"Uh, are you seriously masturbating while I watch?" His cock throbbed. *If she only knew how much I'm into that.*

"Why not?" A coy smirk curved her lips. "It's not every day a hot guy kisses me with an erection."

He crossed his arms. *Definitely not drunk.* "You want help?"

"I thought you weren't that kind of guy?" she drawled.

"If you want my cock, you need to prove your skill set."

She arched an eyebrow. "Kinky. What are you proposing?"

Dylan smirked, licking a fang. "So, what's got you so flustered where you needed a release?"

Abigail looked away, ashamed as she confessed, "I can't get wet."

"Oh?" He marched into the shower, towering over her, arms still crossed. "I can help with that."

She turned her eyes to him; the hunger and lust made him ache. "Are you seriously wearing your pants in the shower?"

"Why not? We're not fucking, are we?" *Now I see it. A short temper and stubbornness. I want to tame her, something about her wild but broken. She wants a rebound, but is too scared to go all-in. Good thing I'm a gambler. And I'm going to go all-in on this bet.*

She glared at the tent between his pants, as if weighing her options. "And how are you ever going to satisfy me without that."

"Is that a challenge?"

A sparkle in his eyes made her grin. "Yes." She pulled her hands away, bracing herself as she leaned back, spreading her legs wide. "I want to see your method of…"

Dylan knelt and ran a tongue from her knee, up her inner thigh. Her breath caught. Her skin was soft and wet under the heat of his hands as they rolled over her hips, upward until they cupped her breasts. His lips wrapped and sucked on one nipple, then moved to the other. Stolen glances made it clear he had her full attention as she moaned, arching so his lips had their fill of her breast.

Releasing her nipple, he pushed his luck further, becoming more intimate. His lips met hers, and he kissed her. She deepened the kiss, the tips of their tongues dancing against each other. At last, he licked into hers, a full-bodied rubbing of tongues as she moaned once more. Her hot fingers glided across his shoulders, before snaking into his hair. Her knees rose higher, her hips daring to rub against his hard cock still imprisoned in his pants.

Her hands slid down his torso, exposing her truest desires.

He pulled away, brushing his thumb over a cheek, down her neck and through the center of her body. She gasped, goosebumps rolling across the valleys of her body as his fingers glided down her slick pussy, rubbing between the swollen folds.

"I fixed your plumbing issue," he announced, smirking.

"Do I get to see what's behind the curtain?" She teased. "Or you still hoping I come first?"

"Something tells me you're used to dealing with guys into tits and ass." He gave her a toothy grin. "But tonight, you just met a man who's all about the pussy."

You have no idea how much I will enjoy making you come, again and again, before I bother to finish myself off.

7

BEDROOM HYMNS

*T*he Devil is about to rock my world.

Dylan's touch made her melt. Abigail's body trembled, and she cursed herself for ruining the chance to have sex with him when he started the shower. His dark eyes had her ensnared, his horns fueling her wanton desires. His fingers glided over her slick pussy, daring to enter her before retreating to her clit. She squealed with the way he rolled over her bean, making her body jolt and tingle.

Why can't it feel this amazing when I touch myself? Is this why they call it the devil's doorbell!

She leaned forward, her rising orgasm tensing her pussy. Her knees pressed into his shoulders, her hands trying to pull him from her.

He slowed, tilting his head at her. "You're close, why stop me?"

"I... I can't." She panted, her embarrassment killing her mood. "When I come, I..."

His brow lowered, and her eyes darted away. "Why the sudden sense of bashfulness?"

Dylan's fingers abandoned her clit, in favor of rubbing the slick opening. "Look, when I come, I..." Her words caught again as his fingers slid inside. She gasped, tightening on his fingers. "D-d-don't, it's just..."

"Just what?" His head bowed, the heat of his breath making her pussy ache with anticipation. "What's your dirty little secret, Angel Abby?"

The devil is about to eat me alive, and I can't even confess about what happens when I come. Come on, just blurt it out!

With a twist of his wrist, his fingers rubbed against a sweet spot, and she panicked. "Dylan don't! I'll squirt!"

He froze, and she looked away, avoiding his face. She squeezed her eyes tight, waiting for him to pull away like so many others had before. Looking back, she had told Bradley about it a week or two ago. His face had twisted into disgust, one she imagined Dylan wearing now. Her body shook with anger and frustration. Cursing it all, cursing the world for giving her such a horrendous flaw.

Of all the things my body does, why that?

Dylan moved closer, his lips tickling her ear as his breath brushed her neck and shoulder like hot wax. "Good. We're in the shower, and I'm feeling lucky. I'm pretty good with slots, so..."

The heat of his lips kissed down her neck, over her collarbone, only stopping to suckle a nipple. His fingers started to rub, stroking in and out, as her legs shook. She arched into the cold glass wall, a stark comparison to the heat of Dylan's body. He released her nipple, leaning back to admire her as their eyes met.

"Relax," he demanded. "I want to see you come, don't hold back."

She bit her lip, eyes tight. *Dammit, I'm just getting more tense.*

"Open your eyes." The command had a dark tone, and it rattled her to meet his gaze. "Good girl. Now, open your legs wider." She followed the provocative instruction, her heart racing. "Now, again. Relax. Lean back, moan and scream if that's what it takes to keep yourself from locking up. I want you to enjoy every touch, every stroke."

He leaned down, never breaking their gaze as he ran his tongue across her clit, slow and hot. Her breath caught, pressing herself against the glass wall as she gripped the edge of the marble bench. A sparkle glinted in his eye, his eyes falling to her wet pussy. She moaned as the heat of his lips wrapped around her bean. He kissed it with passion, making love to it. She tightened on the slow, stroking fingers, tilting her hips.

Closing her eyes, she slowed her breath, enjoying the sensations he gave her. It took everything she had to keep her thighs apart for him. She let go of the bench moaning as she began rocking into him, making him stroke deeper. With each tilt, he'd reward her with another long sucking of her swollen jewel. Her hands wandered down to his head. Fingers brushed against his horns, and she looked down at him with heavy-lidded eyes. Pulling his fingers from her, his hands gripped her inner thighs and pushed her open. Her fingers caressed the horns, and they locked eyes once more.

He's enjoying this, and I want more. I want to come for him.

She gripped his horns, long and devilish. His tongue dove between the folds, his goatee tickling the swollen flesh, making her arch. The hungry slurping and sucking made her pull him into her, the idea he would eat her like dessert added to her arousal. His tongue licked upward, back to her clit flicking and licking it faster. She yelped, abandoning her hold on his head to brace against the bench. His fingers thrust inside her, hard and fast, rubbing the sweet spot from before. Her voice was lost to moaning and screaming, her legs jittering from the rising climax.

Her body tensed. The heat wrapped tight on thrusting fingers. A rush of fluid released. Dylan leaned back his fingers, rubbing harder, increasing the orgasm. His eyes were focused on her pussy, focused on making her come, longer and harder.

A visceral howl escaped her, the last of her reservations broken. Another gush and she could feel it spray like an unkempt water hose.

Dylan's grin only grew.

Oh... holy hell... I've never cum so hard in all...

"Don't stop." He shifted his wrist and another rise and gush hit her. "That's a good girl, keeping cumming for me."

She leaned forward, her body tensing in new ways. The release, freeing and invigorating. His lips met hers, kissing her deeply. Her arms wrapped around his neck, the shower still running and steaming around them. Breaking the kiss, he nibbled her ear, his fingers still stroking her, never slowing, or missing the rhythm that kept her edging on another orgasm.

"I want you." His voice was raw and gruff. "I want to feel you come on my dick."

"Fuck me." She breathed. "Fucking take me to hell and back again. But dammit, fuck me like you mean it."

"As you wish." He bit her ear lobe and goosebumps rattled her body.

His fingers left her as he teased her with his lips, sucking on her ear before kissing her neck. The sound of his pants unzipping made her shudder. She wanted him inside her, wanted to hear him moan, to feel him throb within her. With a thump, his soaked pants hit the shower floor, heavy and wet. Inhaling, she tensed as the bare skin of his hips slid up her wet thighs, the tip of his hard cock pushing against her opening. He halted. Leaning back, his lips left her neck. She stared up, startled by the hesitation, but as their eyes met, he entered her.

Slowly, his thick hard cock filled her until their hips pressed against each other. Those dark eyes peering down at her, his hands bracketing her sides as they hooked her knees. Her legs rose higher on his torso, allowing him to press deeper, knees hung on muscled arms. Abigail's body slid on the marble as he shuffled and redirected their position. The glass had disappeared behind her as he laid her gently on the bench. Grinding against her slowly, she moaned, arching. He lowered atop her, her breasts pressing against his chest.

"You promise to be a good girl?" He huffed, his cock sliding out. "Promise you'll come for me one more time?" Shoving forward, she shrieked with delight.

"Y-yes."

"Promise me Abigail." He rocked his hips with skill, his cock riding in and out of her, teasing her pussy. "Promise you'll not hold back."

"I p-p-promise."

Again, his lips locked with hers. He rocked in and out of her, slow to retrieve, hard and fast to enter her. His hands gripped her ass, tilting her up and she moaned into his mouth. He began to moan with her, she could feel him throbbing inside her, growing harder as his own orgasm neared its peak. The stiffness sent her over the edge. Arching, he captured a nipple between his lips, teasing it with his teeth. She gushed, the heat of her squirting trickling down her ass cheeks. He abandoned her breast. Moaning as he pulled out and rubbed himself. He came across her belly, but she could care less. The orgasm she'd gained was reward enough as she drowned in it.

They both panted as he stumbled back until he leaned his back on the shower wall. "Dammit."

"What's wrong?" she panicked, sitting up.

He had his face covered; horns now vanished. "You're amazing. And I'm in so much trouble."

What's that supposed to mean?

Peeking over his hand, his eyes flowed over her once more and she shuddered. "You feel that too, huh?"

Inhaling deep, Abigail gauged the entire scene. "That raw want. Like I was..." She searched for the word.

"Lucky."

"Y-yea. Something similar. I guess I could say that, but I normally have bad luck." She stood and stepped into the stream of water, shocked it hadn't gone cold. "Yes, lucky definitely describes it."

"We call it the Devil's Luck." He ran his hand over his hair, a smirk on his face. "But I have to be honest, I normally get that high when gambling on something. This is the first time it's been ... sexual."

"Ok... you're talking like this is some sort of paranormal miracle." She lathered her body in his body soap, wondering if she should just buy it for herself when this moment of luck ended. "I may go to church, but I don't necessarily believe in free miracles."

He scoffed. "It wouldn't be so alarming if it weren't for the fact, I recognize the sensation of the power. Like magnets, drawn together. I don't normally enjoy... never mind."

She gave him a cautionary glare. "Never mind what?"

"I'll tell you later if you decide to stick around." He closed the gap between them, reaching for the soap over her shoulder. "And Abigail?"

"Y-yes." Her heart fluttered at the man who'd rocked her world minutes before... so close, *too close, too soon.*

"Don't you ever hold back in bed with me, either."

Is he threatening me?

"You make that sound like we're continuing this in the bedroom."

A soapy finger slid between her thighs, making her lean into him. "If we're as lucky as I think, we will continue this in more than the bedroom."

He pulled away, rinsing off and leaving her alone in the shower. She could breathe again, her mind racing. A shiver rolled through her. The way he touched her, his erotic words haunting and making her body heat by stepping close to her. She'd be lying to think she didn't want one more time with him.

Satisfied, she grabbed a towel and dried herself off. Catching a glance of herself in the mirror, she paused, then smiled. *I've never been with someone who made me feel like a goddess before.*

Wrapping the towel around herself, she wandered into the bedroom and paused.

He was on the bed, naked, waiting for her. "I've decided I'll just share my bed." He gave a devilish smirk, and she couldn't resist smiling. "Can you live with that?"

Shrugging, she sashayed along the bed's edge, the covers thoughtfully pulled back for her. "It's your bed."

"I sleep naked," he warned, nodding at the dresser behind her. "But if you don't, you can borrow my clothes."

"You know..." Abigail let her towel fall to the floor, and she slid into the covers. "I think I might give this a try."

"Oh?" He slid into the covers with her, curving his body around her. "So, do you like being naked with the New Jersey Devil?"

She snaked his arm around her, wanting to be held. "Yea, I like this."

This is how I always imagined feeling—safe and warm, in the arms I could trust.

8

HALO

Dylan slid his arm out from under Abigail, twisting so he hovered over her. Her face was calmer as she slept, a stark difference from the emotions she'd displayed the night before. Smirking, he broke his admiration and moved through the bedroom like a phantom. He left her in a tangle of sheets.

She's so damn beautiful.

Grabbing some items from his dresser, he grabbed his phone and made a call, closing the bedroom door and marched down the hall. The other line rang several times until a familiar voice answered, his excitement unmistakable.

Let's just get this conversation over and done with.

"So," Satch cooed. "How did last night go?"

"None of your business." Dylan scoffed, walking into his kitchen. "What time is the gala?"

"Right!" The sound of a chair squeaking was followed by keys clacking, filling the dead air before he answered, "It's starting at five tonight. Looks like the florist just showed up and stored some of the centerpieces in the spare fridge. That was a good call you made to reorganize the kitchen. The ice sculpture seems to be on the way. Chef Bordeaux says he will have full staff, and a few showing up for stand-by. Did you want to oversee the last of the setup today?"

"Actually, no. I'll let you and Sireena handle that this time. Were you able to convince her to sing for the entertainment? If not, see who else can fill it. In fact, just handle it. I have other shit to do today." Opening the fridge, he grabbed the orange juice, then shut the door. "Can I get an exclusive shopping spree in that shop downstairs? ASAP."

"Which shop?" Satch's chair squeaked again, halting the typing. "You do know there's three of them, right?"

Grabbing a glass from the cupboard, Dylan sighed. "Since when did we have three stores?"

"I'm pretty sure *you* signed off on the paperwork." Satch chuckled, then whispered, "It's for that girl, Abigail?"

Dylan choked on his orange juice. *Damn him...*

"You want to reserve the dress shop, don't you? You're trying to buy your way into her panties." Satch cackled as the choking increased. "Let me guess, you plan on bringing her to the gala tonight? Boy, I wish I could've seen her reject you."

At least, he thinks he won the bet. Let's keep it that way.

Dylan glanced up, meeting Abigail's gaze as she rounded the hallway, using his finger to signal her to remain quiet. "You're right, she wasn't impressed by me at all." She paused, twisting her lips. "Look, I'll text you as soon as you confirm that the store is ready. I want her to be able to shop without intrusion."

Abigail tilted her head and pointed to herself.

Huh, that necklace... Dylan winked, taking down the last sip of his orange juice. *That. Necklace. That. Stone. I know it.*

"Giving her the princess treatment?" Satch quipped, tapping again on the keyboard.

An old story, about never being able to face love again. That's the Devil's Stone. It couldn't be the same one as when I...

"More like giving a princess what she deserves."

Damn family curses and fate. Being a shifter can be annoying. To think, humans get dragged in like the rest of us.

Abigail marched across the living room, dragging the sheet behind her. "Look, I don't need people buying..."

"Got to go, Satch." Panicking, Dylan hung up on him.

Glaring at her, he bit his bottom lip. *They always said, when the time's right, the stone would return to the Devil who earned it. I just didn't know it came with baggage. Granted, sexy baggage that tastes like sweet peach pie.* Memories from last night, the excitement and orgasmic waves haunted him.

"Dylan." She tugged up the sheet, nothing between them except the island countertop. "Look, you don't have to buy me anything. Last night, I was... well, I..."

"You?" Dylan poured himself another glass, lifting an eyebrow. "Last night, yes? Go on..."

"I..." Abigail's eyes fell. "I need to return to Philly. Thank you for letting me crash here, but I need to go home."

"Oh?" He grabbed a second glass and began filling it. "I'll take you there, but you'll have to wait until after I take care of business with my boss tonight. Technically, I should've worked this morning, but I've made arrangements to care for my guest instead."

"R-right. I wouldn't want to be an inconvenience, but you don't have to entertain me. I can just sit here and wait for you. Or in the downstairs bar?"

"That'd be boring for you and me." He chucked the empty jug into the trash. "Besides, I didn't want to show up stag to this event. The boss's daughters are rather ... thirsty."

Abigail searched the air, gathering her thoughts. "Wait, last night, you said you were the chief ... manager?"

"Close." He rounded the counter, as her eyes averted his naked body for the ceiling. "Chief Operating Officer. Part owner, in fact. Tonight, the CEO is having a Gala. I don't intend to stay long, so you'll make the perfect excuse to ditch early. Trust me, I will owe you a favor. Hope you don't ... mind..." He approached, offering her the other glass, leaning into her stare. "You can stare. It won't stop me from staring at you when you drop that sheet."

Abigail blushed.

I guess mulatto girls can turn red after all! How cute!

He spun on his heels, returning to the counter as he gulped down his glass. A smile stretched across his face. Stealing a glance over his shoulder, he caught her gaze. Goosebumps crawled across his skin, the heat of his arousal making him shudder.

"But in all fairness, it's only right if you decide what to wear tonight." He abandoned the glass on the counter. "Sadly, I don't keep spare clothes for women around, but you can borrow my sweatpants and hoodie." Abigail choked on the orange juice as he breezed past her. "I'm pretty sure you don't want to wear the same dress today. Anyhow, it's all still wet from my pants. So, you have any spare clothes to wear downstairs?"

"C-crap!" Panicking, she shuffled in the sheet and chased after him. "Dylan, that is your name, right?"

He paused, allowing her to lead the way. "Yes, Abby?"

There was a pause before she huffed out her frustration. "How can you be so casual about this?"

Dylan cracked a smile. "Can't a man walk around his own apartment naked?"

"Not that." Tugging up the sheet to keep herself covered, she relented, "Me. How can you be so calm about me?!"

He laughed, and her blush deepened. "Last night, I may have brought you to my room, but you didn't have anywhere else to go. If I recall right, you offered to sleep with me in the elevator, I offered to get you a hotel room, then in the shower you asked for my help and how could I say no? It took everything I had to gently turn you down during the shower bit, but..."

"You're right. I did offer." She rolled her eyes before locking with his playful stare. "But...?"

I wonder if she knows. "It's almost like fate brought you here."

She stiffened. "What's that supposed to mean?"

"That necklace." He stepped forward, rolling the stone amulet in his fingers. "You know what this is called, don't you?"

The stone was like a hot coal, but he ignored the searing heat. Its magic vibrated through him, his joints feeling the tinge of electricity, exciting his body. Devil horns, fangs, and even a pointy tail appeared as his body reacted to the direct contact. His dark irises shifted to blood red as they looked at her at last.

"The Devil's Stone," she whispered in awe.

"Do you know the story behind it?" He dropped it, and the shift ended, his eyes dark and devilish features returned to normal.

Her eyes searched his; confusion written on her face. "It's a family heirloom. A lover's gift before he died in the mines."

And there's the explanation. That mine was cursed and turned every man who entered into a devil shifter and every male offspring thereafter. In her case, it's been passed down in the family like a lucky charm, but have they been free of the curse? How are they avoiding the whiplash unless someone put their luck into the stone... could it be?

He shook his head. "It's beautiful, but let's find you a dress for the gala. Ready to go downstairs?" he asked, changing topics.

Perhaps my Devil's Luck is the real deal. Granted it was my father who was cursed, unwilling to get rid of the last stone until his son found it. Unlike him, I was the first to be born a devil.

Dylan walked ahead of Abby, glaring at his fingers, as if they still touched the stone. *A lover's gift. How strange. Just maybe his Devil's luck granted him a wish. Since they closed that mine, there's been no more devils made. Many have shifted and lost their minds, others hunted or killed at birth out of fear and mass hysteria. Honestly, I don't want to be the only Jersey Devil in existence… It's the worst kind of loneliness.*

9

THE DEVIL WEARS A SUIT AND TIE

Abigail did her best to ignore the stares and whispers. Dylan's hoodie swamped her, and she was thankful for the pull string around the waist. He unlocked the store, and she shoved past him. Another chuckle rattled out of him. She stopped, her fingers fumbling the hem of the hoodie as she looked over the dresses once more.

Without customers or the sales associate, the store was silent, and the casino muted.

"Buy anything and everything you want. It's on me." He grabbed a pair of thongs. "That includes underwear for now and later."

"Stop it!" she hissed, tugging the lingerie from his fingers. "You're so embarrassing."

"Me? Embarrassing?" he asked, shocked and amused by this revelation. "I don't find myself embarrassing at all."

"Of course not." She looked at the thongs a moment before tossing them back in the pile.

"Aw, I thought those would look good on you." Pouting, she turned away, hiding her face in the hood. "Seriously, Abby. Don't just buy stuff for today or tonight. Anything you want. You have no idea how big of a favor this is, being my guest at the Gala."

"So you keep telling me," she drawled, heading for the clearance bin, riffling through the selection once more. "Just, let me see if there's anything I consider acceptable."

It kills me. Why is a man this rich and good-looking wanting to pamper me like this? I don't deserve it. I'm only here because I got wasted, searching for a rebound, and missed my bus in the process, while avoiding going home to... She paused, the black cocktail dress from yesterday was in her hand. *I suppose I should heed the initial advice and just enjoy myself. Mourn the loss of my engagement, not that fucking scumbag Bradley.*

Circling back to the lingerie section, she paid no heed to his curious eyes. "That was in clearance?"

She ignored him, looking for her size in bras. *Dammit, his pants soaked everything I came here with. It was so damn awkward, walking through that crowd, knowing how naked I was under this.*

She smacked a mischievous hand from her ass. "Stop it. Not here," she grumbled, pulling a bra free, then turning to the underwear section.

Dylan frowned. "You said the same thing on the elevator. No fun."

"To be honest, I didn't think you'd pick a dress like that one. Doesn't seem your style."

"It's not," she confessed, heading for the fitting room before he could see her grab the thongs he'd picked out. "Taking a friend's advice to let loose and have some fun. I should've done this yesterday. I'm not wasting my second chance."

"Good advice, and I like where this is going." He leaned against the wall, just outside the door, his voice soothing her nerves.

"Only thing you like about it is a second chance to…" She snapped her jaw closed as she wiggled out of his hoodie and sweatpants. *What am I saying! That I plan on fucking him again? Why can't I just keep my mouth shut!*

"Second chances are my specialty," he chuckled.

Again, she focused on the task at hand. *There's always something sexy about sliding on a lacy black thong and matching bra.* A smile came to her face. She peeked at herself in the mirror before sighing. Grabbing the cocktail dress up, she slipped it on. It flowed off her hips like velvety waterfalls of fabric. Adjusting her breasts into the top, she paused, catching something shiny. A golden embroidery bordered the halter top and chased down the back center. Here she hummed to herself, a small train exploding in a grand firework design where the two-sides met as one.

It's prettier than I realized.

Reaching behind herself as she attempted to tie up the back. Her arms and wrists ached from the effort as she cursed her inflexible body. Another growl of frustration exploded and a knock at the door startled her. Her heart pounded against her chest making it ache.

Shit, how'd I forget he was circling just outside the door?

"You need help with lacing up the back?" he cooed.

He was hoping for this moment.

She cracked the door ajar. "No funny business."

"You act like I haven't seen what's under that." He lifted his eyebrows, and she let him in. "Sorry, you make it easy to get a rise out of you. Consider it a compliment from me, I don't indulge in flirting like this often."

Abigail stiffened, catching the sincere expression on his face as the heat of his fingers laced the back of the dress. "You call that flirting?"

As his fingers worked up the pattern of cross-stitched ribbon, he caught her stare in the reflection. "It's working to get a grin out of you on occasion, isn't it? That flushed look is quite sexy after all." He tightened the top and vanished out of the room, door closing.

Abigail stood there, staring at where he should've been, should have stayed and it felt … empty. *Painfully empty and cold without him there.* Snapping out of it, she swirled before the mirror, running her hands down her sides. The dress was stunning. It may not have caught her eye but seeing it on her frame, she understood why DeeDee had suggested it. She filled it in all the right places. Satisfied, she tugged the ribbon knot free and wiggled out.

This will be the dress for tonight but until then… She looked at his hoodie and sweatpants and laughed. *Second time this weekend I've had to shop here in sweats.*

"Hey, Dylan. Did you mean it when you said I can buy more than one?" she shouted through the door. "And am I allowed to wear the merchandise out the door?"

"Yes, to both. We'll leave a list, or you can settle up and add it on my tab later."

Abigail flinched; he sounded *sad?* "In that case, to be fair…"
"Fair?"

Yes, sad. "Pick out something for me. Something you like."

"You sure about that? You didn't seem to care for my choice in panties." He laughed and she smiled as she placed the dress back on its hanger and worked the wrinkles out.

"Go pick something." There was silence.

The minutes ticked by; a chill rattling over her. She reached for the knob and stopped. *I'm in my underwear! Where the hell did he go?* Turning to the dress, she shook her head. *That's for tonight.* Grabbing the hoodie, she pulled it back on and tugged it down. It was every bit as long as the sundress she wore yesterday, and she laughed as she ventured out of the fitting room.

"Dylan?" The store lay silent, empty from where she stood.

I have to confess something to myself. Her heart pounded in her ears, her blood rushing. *Every part of me wants to stay here with him. It's not the money. It's not that he's so damn handsome, and dammit he looks good in a suit and tie but...* She tip-toed, circling around the racks of clothes wondering where he could be. *There's something devilish about him that just makes me want him more and more with each passing minute. The idea we might part ways tonight makes me want to...* Her eyes began to water.

"Where are you?"

Again, silence and she swallowed. Someone knocked on the shop door and she hid behind a nearby rack. They moved on and she could breathe again. *I'm being ridiculous. He had to do something for work.* The aching in her chest only added to the weight of her depression. Staring at her feet, she marched right back into the fitting room, slamming the door.

"That's exactly what I was hoping you'd be wearing."

Her head jerked up. He'd snuck into the fitting room in her distraction. She couldn't contain the smile. Rushing her, his lips locked with hers, the kiss hungry and passionate. Her tongue dove into the warmth of his mouth and her body heated with the memories of what it had done, had tasted of her last night.

His hands glided up her thighs and under his hoodie. The throb of want rattled through her and his shoulders shuddered as she let herself be pinned against the door. It rattled under their fast and desperate movements. His fingers looped into the thong and his grin broke their kiss.

"I thought you didn't like these."

"They weren't for me." He started to slide them slowly and teasingly off her, his lips leaving a burning trail down her leg. "And they were supposed to be a surprise for later."

"Oh I'm surprised." She lifted one foot then the other.

A tongue chased the trail back up the inside of her leg and she gasped. He shouldered the leg as he crested over her knee and up her thigh, never slowing to reach the prize swollen and wet. *I've never gotten so hot and bothered in my life from a look, a kiss, or a...* A squeal erupted from her, his lips wrapping around her clit. He sucked long and hard, his tongue circling slowly and purposefully. *He's been thinking about this all day.*

A hand rolled up the center of her torso and her breathe caught in her throat. She tensed, an orgasm coming on quick if he kept instigating her body in this way. *Should I stop him? What about...* He changed tactics as his fingers slid under the bra, groping her breast. The suckling had ended, and his tongue lapped up everything her pussy offered. She moaned, giving way to the waves of pleasure rolling through her. Her leg shook under the pressure, and she was failing to brace herself against the door.

Don't let this end... I don't want him to stop... I don't want to leave him.

10

DEVILS DON'T FLY

Dylan pulled away, his cock hard from teetering her on the edge of a monstrous orgasm. He let her leg slide off as she hummed against the door. He shed his clothes, fast and eager. Searching a pocket, he found a condom and she laughed. Shrugging he rolled it onto his throbbing erection. She started to pull off his hoodie and he rushed her once more. Lips hot against his own as he kissed her deeply. Her breast heaved against him; he pinned her hard against the door.

After a blind search, he found her wrists and pinned them up above her head. Compared to him, she seemed small and delicate. A single hand could pin her crisscrossed arms and her kiss pressing back told him she would let him. His thigh slipped between her own, wet from her building arousal. Breaking the kiss, he licked and nibbled at her ear. Her body shook, her pussy grinding against his leg as she whimpered.

"The moment you walked out of my room wearing this, I've wanted to fuck you." Breathless, she moaned as he kissed her neck. "Don't you dare take it off."

His leg shifted, opening her to receive him. He slid in slowly, soaking in her heavy-lidded look. Licking a fang, he realized the stone glowed from under the fabric, and it egged him to keep going. His free hand slid down to grip her ass, pushing further inside her before slowly grinding against her. They both moaned enjoying the slow, deep thrusting.

She lifted her leg up on his hip and he began thrusting harder and faster. The way her body shook in anticipation of the inevitable orgasm only added to his own. To know he could bring her to the edge, so close that she grew wet with each stroke of his cock inside her.

"You promise you won't hold back, right?" he huffed, goosebumps rattling him.

"I promise." She huffed, shifting into him, making him throb inside her.

"Tell me, my dear Abby, my beloved Angel..." He suckled her ear, inhaling her intoxicating scent. "Tell me what you desire?"

"I want..." He started kissing down her neck, enjoying how easily each touch disrupted her words. "Want... D..."

"I can't hear you." His voice gruff as his hand slid down between their bodies. "Speak up."

"Desire..." She gasped for air. "I des..."

His fingers found her clit. The touch making her pussy tighten on his cock and he moaned in her ears. He nuzzled around to her other ear. Licking up her neck, kissing and suckling as he wore a devilish grin. Fanged and wild, he enjoyed the game of cat and mouse he played with her pleasure and her voice.

"Dylan." His name fell with provocative want, and he throbbed once more.

Pulling from the nest of her hair, he leaned back catching her gaze. "Yes?"

She laughed, his grip on her arms letting go. Abigail cupped his jaw, and he soaked up her smile. *It's so beautiful. And to think, it's only meant for me. Who could be so blind to give you up? I guess the only heart breaking when you leave will be my own.* He heaved a sigh, searching her face. *Would you stay if I asked you to? Would you stay even after confessing what I am?*

"You asked for what I desired." She gave him a peculiar look.

"And I would give you the world if I could." He furrowed his brow. "So what do you desire most?"

"You, silly. I desire ... Dylan."

His smile fell away, *did I just have a seizure?* It wasn't the answer he had expected. Not in this moment of sexual play.

She pressed her lips against his and he fumbled backward. They crossed the tiny span of the fitting room until his back locked with the cold mirror. *She can't want me. She shouldn't want me ... even though it's what I wanted; it just makes this so much worse.* Her lips abandoned their play and the hot silk of them started down his neck, over his collarbone. The trail was slow and agonizing, like a ribbon brushing against his skin, teasing as it fell to the place that throbbed with want.

Should we even be going this far if I intend to make this more? If she wants more than this weekend of lust, if she feels like I do and wants to see where we can go from here...

Her fingers grabbed his hard cock, yanking the condom off. Moaning, he closed his eyes, bracing his arms on the sides of the tiny room. The urge to rush her, to press his dick between those fleshy petals tantalizing. A hot blanket of her breath made him groan and throb once more. Her lips at last kissed along his length. First one side, then the other and back again. He bit his lip as her tongue circled the tip.

I've never felt so alive with someone. Is this what it means to start falling for someone. If that happens, it'll only mean ... danger. Yes, she'll be in danger with me and with this otherworld I live in. It's not frowned upon for shifters and humans to be together, but I'm involved with so many predators...

At last, he peered down at her, licking his lips. She ran her tongue, firmly from base to tip on the underbelly of his cock and he moaned again. Her eyes looked at him, and she paused. She stroked his length before a look of contemplation passed on her face.

I might just lose control of that part of me I hate so much. The part I haven't been able to keep secret since she stepped foot in this place.

"I know you keep saying this is who you are, but..." She motioned to her forehead, and he realized the horns had crept forward yet again. "Is that make up or another illusion?"

"Dammit." He eyed the mirror behind him; they were large and every bit of eight inches long.

"How does that even happen? I mean, they look so real. When did you slip them back on?" She licked the tip of his dick, teasing him. "Don't make me tease you until you confess. It's a little sexy so..."

"That's just mean," he huffed. *Son of a bitch. I can't do this. Not to her. Not when she deserves better. She deserves the truth.* Dylan pulled her away and she looked up in confusion from the hard shift from sex to serious discussion time. "Look, Abigail, I'm a shifter. Touch them. They're the real deal and if I lose control, it will only get ... *uglier*. Horns, tail, wings as black as night: these are who I am."

"You're a shifter? Like in those romance novels?" She gave a nervous laugh before sputtering, "You're joking, right?" Her smile faltered. "Please tell me you're joking, Dylan?"

Dammit, if I want her to stay, I need her to understand what it means to be with me.

"Yea, well, those are based on more fact than you think. Half the time the authors are shifters themselves." Dylan averted his eyes from her as he sank to the floor. *What a buzz-kill this is going to be.* "I'm not completely human. We still don't understand it all ourselves, but there's a level of magic involved. Curses and blessings have all been blamed. Legends and mythology, hell even history has left clues. Look, I'm wild about you. I can't keep this from happening around you," he pointed to the horns, "and I can't keep ignoring it and neither can you, though I appreciate the way you've handled it so far."

Abigail broke away, adding space between them as the weight of the situation hit her. "Last night I told myself it was the alcohol. Even this morning I thought maybe, maybe a dream and I wasn't quite awake all the way or ... it can't be."

"We both know you weren't that drunk. Denial is normal." He refused her gaze, accepting the inevitable end. *I don't want to see that kind of hurt in those eyes. Rather break it now, it only gets messier the longer I keep this to myself.* "So, before I dare take this any further... I needed you to know. To see what I am. Just, feel free to hate me but don't go blasting it to the press." He swallowed, the anxiety of it all tight in his chest as he covered his face. *I've spent my entire life avoiding this moment. It's only happened once before, and it ruined me. What the hell was I thinking. I knew I'd fall for her the moment I saw her at the slots. Fuck!* "Forget everything. Let's take you back to Philly. I'm sorry I strung you along-"

"STOP!" Her shriek jolted him.

Pulling his hand down his face, he dared to look her way, but she buried her face in the sleeves of his hoodie. "Look, the deal holds. Pick what you want, and I'll take you home. You don't worry about the gala it's..."

"Just … let me enjoy this a little longer." At first, he wasn't sure what he heard. "Let me stay with you a little longer. Don't make me go back there."

He blinked, the tears glazing her eyes. "I didn't mean to hurt you. I didn't want to make you cry."

"These aren't from you." She sniffled, her voice shaking. "This is for what waits for me in Philly."

A profound look hit his face. "Why did you run away?"

She laughed, "Like I said, he fucked the organ player. My ex-fiancé is the pastor, and he fucking cheated on me." Burying her face back into the sleeves of his hoodie, she forced the words out. "The man threatened to turn the whole congregation on me for catching them, and here you are rewarding me for weaseling my way to your bed. I thought it fitting I was dragged to a casino and in the bed of the Devil. At first it just seemed like a lucid dream, even a drunken dream. You've been nothing but kind and you fucking make me feel like a person again. Like I matter."

"You do matter." He crawled closer and forced her hands down. "In the flitting time we've been together you have caught me off guard on more than one occasion. You're funny and brave when you want to be. At times outspoken, but I hate seeing you hurt and hiding away within yourself. I want to see more of these glimpses, more of that smile … that you give me and me alone." He thumbed her bottom lip, his eyes lingering on them before wiping a tear from her cheek. "Fuck the asshole who made you doubt who you are."

"I feel like I'm using you." She shook her head. "I'm a horrible person. I deserve every bit of this."

Her words made his heart sink. *And here I thought I was … using her, getting what I deserved by letting her go.* "So what. You used me for your rebound. Sleeping with the devil seems like a great way to get back at a cheating pastor but…"

She rushed forward, arms wrapping around him, her voice desperate as it vibrated into him. "I'm falling for you. I don't want to leave, and I don't know what's right or wrong anymore. I don't know if it's good luck or bad luck that brought me to you."

You're not alone, my Angel. I'm starting to wonder too.

MY CHURCH

"**O**k, Angel." Abigail was forced to her feet and the sweatpants shoved in her hands. "I'll loan you some of my Devil's Luck in that case."

Can he even do that? Is this a shifter thing? Even after confessing I'm using him, then...

"You're not mad at me?" She looked at him, bewildered as he shuffled on his pants.

"As long as you're not upset that I'm a shifter, I think we can call this even." He winked at her, and she began to put the pants on. "Let's get you what you need, a proper shower, and I'll pay the salon to do your hair and makeup. I want you to be the sexiest thing walking into that gala tonight, if you're up for the task."

If I'm being honest, I don't quite understand what being a shifter means. What I do understand is he's the biggest playboy bachelor with deep pockets in Jersey and... Abigail's self-esteem wavered again. "It's still a pig, even if you put make up on it."

He backed her against the door again, whispering in her ear. "Call me shallow, but I only fuck pretty women."

Arousal washed over her, he refused to let her shove him away. "You can't mean that."

"Why else would I be in this fitting room with you and not out on the casino floor on the prowl, Abby." Her heart jolted at the statement. "Come on. Let me show you what you can have if you want it bad enough."

She laughed. "Are you tempting me?"

"Maybe." He pulled away, his eyes glowing red as the horns receded.

Abigail left it at that. She had aired her confession, but Dylan seemed unphased by it. *Motivated at the thought of it.* As she gathered the dress and lingerie, he encouraged her to grab a few more things just as the sales associate from before came through the door. She smirked, seeing her with him and when Dylan looked away gestured her kudos. Apparently, this was the ultimate prize for anyone on the rebound, but it didn't stop the guilt knotting in her stomach.

Returning to the penthouse suite, the silence and stolen glances continued. Their discussion in the midst of lust and shame inside that tiny fitting room had built an invisible wall between them. Room service came and went, dropping off finger foods. He had gone ahead of her to shower and when she noticed he was done; he had disappeared into his office. Biting her lip, she went about her own business, the apartment unbearably silent and lonesome.

Is this how he normally spends his day in this place? It seems like a miserable existence. Sobering in fact, compared to downstairs.

Wiggling on the sexy black lace lingerie, she avoided the mirror. She couldn't afford to lose what little confidence she had left. *I'm going to a big business gala for the first time, but can*

I even pull this off? Sliding the dress on, she flustered. *Dammit, I can't tie up the back on my own.*

"Here." His voice startled her as the heat of fingers tickled against her back. "After I get you tied up, Angel, we'll head downstairs for some pampering for you. Have you ever had someone professionally do your make up before?"

"N-no." She glimpsed at the mirror, at his stern face. "Is everything ok?"

"Yea." When the last knot was tied, he leaned into her ear. "As long as you stay with me tonight. Just one more night."

He thinks I am to leave immediately. Did I want to leave tonight? Do I ever want to leave? What do I want?

"But you can tell me no." He broke away, and she grabbed his arm. "Yes?"

"I... would love to stay tonight too." The beating of her heart thumped in her chest like a racing horse. "Please let me stay."

He laughed, the features of his face softened, and the smile returned. "Of course."

There's nothing he hadn't handled. As soon as she passed into the salon, a flock of attendants rushed her into a chair and began their work. She would have asked them a million questions, but every time she opened her mouth, they fussed for her to stay still. Make up meant to follow instructions and give the reigns of her own face and lips to the harpy who painted her face with makeup brands she'd never seen in her local grocery store. Her hair on the other hand, was at the mercy of a gentleman who doused her in compliments of how well-kept it was and thanking her for braving to go all natural.

The minutes dragged; she lost track of the time and surely a good hour or more had passed by the time the two attendants pulled away from her. They had her stand now, no mirror in sight as they adjusted how the dress fit her, going as far as redoing the lacing in the back. Having a woman do it instead of Dylan made her face heat. Granted, she couldn't deny how the dress hugged her more comfortably after the tugging and shifting of fabric.

"Now let's have a look. Tell us what you think." The makeup artist walked her to an array of mirrors.

Abigail gasped. "It doesn't even look like me," she muttered at the princess before her.

"Come now, we can only bring out what's already there." The hair stylist chuckled, joining them. "Dylan said he wanted you to look like royalty, how'd we do?"

"A-amazing." Swallowing, she fought the urge to cry. "I feel … spoiled."

"Dylan doesn't do this for girls normally." The mutter made her blink. "Let's hope he approves or I'm out of the job."

"It's perfect, Gretel." Dylan's voice had them twisting in his direction as one. "And that smile on your face says you approve."

"It's amazing. They're amazing." She rushed him, hugging him.

"Careful, or you'll get makeup on my jacket. It's too soon for that." He spun, hiding his face from her as he hooked her arm. "But we're late. Mr. Morozov is at the table already and blowing up my phone."

"Oh no." Abigail held onto him tightly, afraid of tripping in the heels she had picked out. "I'm so sorry, this is my fault."

"The hell it is. I already told you I planned on you being the centerpiece in this gala." Dylan had pulled her through the casino and across to the convention center area. "This is all me."

Anxiety crept up as the butlers at the door waved them through. The ballroom was enormous. A grand chandelier hung from the center as columns of white and gold decorated the walls. She scanned the room of extravagantly dressed guests. Dylan nodded and waved as he passed them, stating names as he went and never losing pace. *He knows all these people.*

"Ah, Mr. Morozov!" They at last came to a stop and her feet ached from the trip they took across the hotel. "Sorry, for the delay. You know how it is, waiting on a lady."

Abigail gave him a death glare. Then the large mountain of an old man burst into laughter.

"From the look in her eyes, it's your fault she ran so late," he said in a heavy Russian accent, standing to his full monstrous height. "Pleasure to meet you." He took her hand and gave it a kiss. "And you are?"

"A-abigail." His eyes were so pale blue, the irises seemed almost white. "Nice to meet you?"

"Well, sit!" He gestured and Dylan nodded. "Come, they should be serving any moment."

"Where's Yvette and Satch?" Dylan's glare grew dark at the empty chairs.

"Hell, if I know. Neither will take my call or reply to a text." A thin man sat beside Mr. Morozov, though similar eyes, his accent was American. "He better show or have a damn good excuse for being late."

"So!" Dylan's voice boomed, rattling everyone at the table. "How's that leg of yours, Ghetti?"

The thin man abandoned his cell phone on the table and leaned back in the chair. "I'm out of the cast, so I can't complain."

"Wow, it's only been thirty days or so, right?" Dylan seemed intrigued by this news as servers brought salads to their table. "I didn't realize you heal fast."

Mr. Morozov laughed in a big rumble. "You forget, we come from a wilder past than your own. We still retain a lot of the ancestral traits. We didn't derive from a curse, speaking of which my dear business partner..." he pointed to Abigail's necklace "... isn't that a Devil's Stone?"

From under the table, Dylan's hand found hers and squeezed it tight. "You amaze me sometimes. I never pick up on magic like you do."

"He cheats," grumbled Ghetti, staring begrudgingly at the two empty spots. "It's our sense of smell that does most of the work."

Chuckling, Mr. Morozov took a bite of salad. Abigail squeezed Dylan's hand again and brought it across her lap. The man's eyes picked her apart, and the words from before: *I'm a shifter,* sent goosebumps over her. *These aren't humans. They're shifters like Dylan... no. This man is something more menacing, older even. What have I gotten myself into?*

Dylan leaned into her, whispering, "Don't get scared, he can smell that too. I'm here. No harm will befall you, my Angel."

"Abigail." She jerked, hearing her name from Mr. Morozov's lips. "Where on earth did you find this amazing trinket? Pawn shop? Thrift store? No. Maybe an antique shop?"

She forced a smile, glancing at Dylan to reaffirm if she should let that information out of the bag. "My ancestor. It's an old family heirloom."

His fork clanked loudly on the plate. He glared at the amulet, then at Dylan, eyes wide.

What in the hell just happened? Did I say something wrong? Is Dylan in some sort of trouble bringing me here? Will I even live to see Philly again with a fiery stare like that?

12

ANGEL OF SMALL DEATH

"**A**bby." Dylan shook her hand from his and squeezed her thigh. "Looks like we have business to discuss. Forgive me, but can you excuse us for a moment."

Dammit, he knows about that legend too. This won't go well. He's gonna talk me out of keeping her ... but I don't even know if she'll really stay with me.

"S-sure." He stood, pressing a soft kiss on her lips. "Did I do something wrong?"

"No, dear." Mr. Morozov stood, giving her a sincere smile. "You've done nothing wrong. This is about ... business."

Dylan turned, marching shoulder to shoulder with the mountain of a Yeti shifter. He hated being around him, the man was smart and had lived over two centuries from what he could pinpoint. Morozov didn't slow down once. Before long they were in the elevator headed to the offices upstairs. Dylan couldn't keep his heart still. *Something isn't right.*

"Where'd you find her." It wasn't a question; this was a demand.

"She came to the casino on the rebound last night." He swallowed. "I didn't notice the necklace until this morning ... after ... well."

"I see." The doors opened, halting Satch and Yvette's laughing.

"D-Daddy." Yvette paled and she grabbed Satch's hand. "We were on our way down."

Mr. Morozov inhaled deeply. "You better put on more perfume and cologne. If Ghetti smells what you two were doing up here on your desk," he shot a wild look to Satch who averted his eyes, "I assure you the gala will come to a halt."

"Yes sir." Satch pushed past them, dragging Yvette as he muttered to Dylan, "Good luck."

The doors shut and Mr. Morozov turned, cupping Dylan's shoulders with heavy hands. "You do know I've hated how you handled this curse."

"Yea, I know." Dylan smirked, it was the reason he'd been shunned and told to stay away from other Devil shifters. "Ex-communicated for tempting the Devil's Luck."

And no one knows where the rest went ... the whole ten or so that remained after what I did as a child.

"I can't lie. Placing a bet on the fact you would be able to beat the full turn by betting your luck against it. Tell me, did you lose at the roulette table yet?"

"Yea, the night she walked in here." Dylan brushed the monstrous hands off and marched toward his office. "But I've been struggling for a few days to keep the horns down."

"I didn't think any of them existed." Mr. Morozov gave chase, spinning Dylan back to look him in the eyes.

He shrugged at the old man. "I knew that old mine closed, but to think not every stone had been returned. The girl's lucky to even have a Devil's Stone and I think..."

"Not the fucking stone, Dylan." He gave him a bewildered look and started laughing. "You didn't notice?"

"Notice what?" *What the hell has this senile Yeti noticed about her I didn't? Shit, I fucked her, have seen her naked, tasted her ... what the hell is he going on about?*

"Holy shit." He held his forehead, pacing the floor. "I don't know if I should tell you. Does she know?"

"That ... I'm a devil shifter?" Frustration seeped forward. "Of course, she knows, I told her."

"Oh hell." He froze, staring into space collecting his thoughts. "She doesn't know, does she?"

"Know what? She knows the story about the stone, she knows I'm a shifter..."

"That she's half a fucking Angel." Mr. Morozov scoffed, shaking his head in disbelief.

Angel ... is an Angel. It was a pet name. He's lost it.

"A what?" Dylan closed the gap. "What are you talking about?"

Laughter rolled out of Mr. Morozov, his gut shaking. "Holy fuck. The Devil fucked an angel half breed and didn't even notice?"

Dylan squinted, his mind stumbling and fighting over itself. "Angels don't exist."

He's crazy. They laughed at me at Brightwater over this question about an Angel shifter.

"Yea, they do. They're like an urban legend, but dammit, I've met one before during the crusades." He whistled, the laughter continuing. "Oh, boy. So she probably doesn't know. Their kind don't mix blood often, boy is someone upstairs in trouble for that one. Dammit, Dylan, that's a lucky streak worthy of legendary status."

Fuck being legendary! If I sent this poor girl's life down this path, shit! Half Angel? What does that even mean? How could she even go all this time not knowing?

"Are you implying I put this into motion?" Covering his face, he paced a few times in panic. "I made that bet, what, when I was a kid. And I stuck by it because once a devil makes a bet, even as a kid, it sticks."

"Did you ask for her birthday?" he offered.

"No, we started last night being a one-night stand and then..."

"Tasted like a peach, didn't it?"

Dylan's face sobered of all emotion. "How would you know?" *Why would he know about that?*

"They say when you find a good match, it's like the sweetest fruit. It's called forbidden fruit for a reason, they don't have to be a shifter for it to happen and there can be more than one girl that does it for you, but it's hard when you made a bet on a dev-il's luck." Another wave of laughter, the rumbling like a distant storm, menacing and frightening. "Wait until I share this with..."

"Don't you dare!" In an instant Dylan changed. Horns black as night pushing ten inches tall, a pointed red tail snaking behind him, and large black feathered wings flaring out. "Don't you tell anyone!"

"Oh, we're serious about her, are we?" There was a sparkle in his eye. "Ok, ok... I won't tell anyone. Wanted to see if you plan on letting her go so easily."

You dick. You needed to know if this was the real deal.

Snorting steam from his nostrils, Dylan shook off the shift and threw off the ripped overcoat. "Dammit. How could she not know?"

"Because a devil hasn't given her, her wings." He followed Dylan into his office where he grabbed a spare coat. "Or so the legend goes. Look, the Devil Stones made humans devils. But an angel—or someone the blood of angels—would be immune, but it brings them bad luck, or in this case, brings them into the luckiest devil in the whole world. I didn't just go into business because you were good at what you do. You couldn't lose no matter how hard you tried."

He shoved on the coat, still fuming. "Look, I need to go down there and discuss this with her. She needs to know. I've got to get her to give up that damn necklace, but... to never know."

What kind of life is that?

"Go get her. She's lucky enough to have found you." He snorted. "Maybe the stone was responsible for that much. Maybe it's never been unlucky."

"It's fate that we met." Dylan gave Mr. Morozov one last look and ran for the elevator. "Thanks!"

The elevator never felt so damn slow. He exploded into the stretch between stores, weaving with practiced skill through the casino floor and came to a halt as he bumped into someone. They dropped their phone, and he realized the pandemonium unfolding behind him. The gala was filled with screeches. The Morozov siblings were wrecking the event in record time and he paled.

"Dylan!" Satch picked his phone up and flashed a picture. "Did this guy just throw a bikini in the fire? He did, didn't he?"

He smacked the phone from Satch's hand. "I don't give a shit, where the fuck is Abby?"

"Oh?" He turned Dylan around and they disappeared into the casino floor crowd. "So her ex-fiancé the preacher marched in and took her?"

"FUCK!" He broke from Satch, charging for the lobby.

Satch shouted after him. "I'm leaving early to pick up Bif and his girl from the forest! Good luck boss!" A trail of black feathers floated to the ground in Dylan's wake. "Oh hell, I'm not staying to see how this ends. The Devil's about to explode."

Please don't take her! I need her! She needs me!

We ... need each other.

13

DEVIL'S BACKBONE

"**G**et your hands off me." At last, Abigail broke from Pastor Bradley's hand at the edge of the lobby. "I'm not going back to Philly. Especially not with you!"

"Come on. You're making a show of this." Sweat trickled down his temple, still dressed in his clerical clothing.

He left right after the last sermon today, didn't he?

"Everyone in the congregation wanted to know where you went." His anger added friction in her core.

"Of course, they did." She shuffled backward, disbelief gripping her. *Why wouldn't they ask?* "Did you tell them why?"

His face reddened, a wild look in his eyes. "I told them you were at home sick."

He blames me for this.

"Until DeeDee spoke up."

"DeeDee?" Abigail's eyes widened. "But she never goes to church on Sunday!"

This man's looking at me as if he caught me on that baptism table.

"I know, and when she said you were stuck here at the casino... Abigail, I was embarrassed. How could you humiliate me like that before the entire congregation! People are starting to ask *me* what *I* did!" He marched toward her, and she kept the gap between them, the vein pulsing on his forehead. "You have to come home with me. Tammy's waiting in the car. This is ridiculous for a Pastor's fiancée..."

"EX-Fiancée." Abigail's rage had finally crested. "I didn't fuck the organ player, asshole. Go to hell!"

She spun around and ran full steam into the sea of casino patrons. Tears threatened, and she could hear his steps heavy behind her. *This is crazy! He cares more about his reputation than what the hell happened!* She kicked off the heels abandoning them in her wake, hiking the dress up to allow her legs to take wider strides in order to properly run. Her feet struck the casino carpet with heavy thuds matching her heartbeat. Pivoting to the right then left, she looked like she was running bases in a baseball game.

Thank you for little league, you finally came through for me! Squeezing her eyes tight, she refused to slow down. *Dylan! I need you! Don't let him take me from you! Damn my luck!*

Another pivot to miss the Blackjack table, and she smashed into someone, their arms wrapping around her tight.

"Let me go!" She shrieked, panic filling her. *I need to find...*

"Abigail." Dylan's voice snapped her eyes open, his eyes glowing red. "You didn't leave."

"Don't let him take me." A tear slid down her cheek, body shaking, the thought frightening. "I can't. He's not the one I love. Dylan, I love..."

"ABIGAIL!" A voice roared in the crowd, chills snaking up her spine.

She gripped onto Dylan's coat, pressing into him. *I'll never let you go!* He tightened his hold and twisted, as if looking for an escape. He froze and pulled her from him, locking eyes. That devilish smirk on his face, the horns starting to peak out of his forehead. *A shifter, a devil. And he loves me, and I love him.*

"Do you trust me?" He pulled her through another crowd and under the caution tape, through the tarps that had barricaded guests from a section of the casino. "He's going to look here too, but..."

Her stomach knotted. *I can't hide.* She stumbled past him to lean on a roulette table in defeat. "I don't ever want to go back to Philly. Let me stay here with you, Dylan. I know it's a crazy request but..."

"Yes." His answer fell hard in the air between them as he tossed his coat on the table. "You *should* stay here with me. Now, about our current situation. I have a devilish solution for you, my Angel."

She twisted to face him, his tie already slipping from his neck as he started to undress.

"I'll do anything to stay with you... what are you doing?"

"Promising the Devil like that is a dangerous thing." He unbuttoned his shirt and it fell to the floor revealing the rips in the backside. "What if I demand more than what you can give me, Abby?"

Her eyes lingered on the shirt with black feathers tangled in the threads. Swallowing, a wave of desire and excitement hit her. *The horns, he said they were real... but he said...* A heat stirred in her, anger and anxiety drowning under love and lust.

"What happened to your shirt?" She marveled, exhilaration bursting through her veins. "Dylan, what are you planning to do to me?"

"Fuck you." He declared, sucking the side of his cheek before closing the gap between them. "Will you fuck the Devil right here, right now?"

Abigail eyed the tarps behind him, the only thing shielding them from the rest of the casino and the crowds of people whose shadows made it ruffle as they passed. *He did say Bradley would find us.* His hand started tugging the dress further up, his knee pressing between her thighs. Her breath caught, heart beating fast and hard. *He's serious. He wants to do this, but...* Her mind and body struggled with one another. *If he found us, like I found them.* A heat of arousal rolled over her as she backed up and found herself pinned between him and a roulette table. *Is it wrong, wanting him to catch us?*

"What if I can't keep quiet?" She eyed his lips as they came closer to her own, all her want hitting her at once. *I was hoping to finish what we started in the fitting room. Why not here and now?* "What if someone hears us?"

"Not even worried about that." The stone at her neck began glowing. "You're the one who likes doing this sort of thing in public places, Ms. I-used-live-the-wild-clubbing-life. Screwing guys in the bathrooms, back alleys, fitting rooms, and now you can add casino to your naughty list."

Dylan kissed her, deeply and passionately. She leaned her weight onto the table, wrapping her arms around his neck. Their tongues wrestling with one another, rubbing hot and wet as they moaned into each other. The way he made her feel, her body alive with lust like never before. *How could I ever say no to this?* She ground against his thigh, flashes of how he felt inside her making her want him. He pulled away and before she could fuss, his hands raced up her legs to pull the black thong off once more.

"Again?" He lifted an eyebrow, the devilish grin with the red eyes and black horns making her shudder with anticipation. "If I didn't know better, you lied when you said I had bad taste."

"Never said that. Just told you how embarrassing it is to see you riffle through a bucket of lacy thongs." She laughed, *even in a moment as wild and crazy as this he manages to get me to laugh. Every fear gone; every desire pulled out to the open just for him to enjoy.* "You paid for them; you can take them back any time you want."

"Just so you know, I'm partial to black, especially lace." He began unbuckling his pants, pulling out his erection and her heart skipped a beat.

"Why's that?" She glanced at the tarp as it moved under the air vent, the excitement adding to the throb of her provocative want. "Ex-girlfriend?"

"No." His eyes glowed in the dim lighting, for the first time everything about him screamed *devil.* "Because they remind me of these."

Like magic, Dylan's black wings exploded behind him. Abigail covered her mouth, eyes widened, marveling at the extraordinary sight. They blocked her view of the tarps, so black she could've mistaken them for the night sky. He gave them one flap, the wind from them slamming into her to confirm they were indeed the real deal. She reached to touch one over his shoulder but recoiled. *How could I be so careless.*

He gripped her wrist, angling her hand until her fingertips touched his feathers. "Please don't ever pull away from me, from them."

Her heart fluttered. "They're soft and ... warm."

Nuzzling her, his voice deep as he whispered, "You're the first to touch them."

How far have you let me into your life to be so reckless? To take all the risk on betting I would stay with you, would keep quiet, and ... accept this of all things?

Before she could say anything, his lips were back on hers. They travelled down her neck, and she grew wet. The heat of his hand plunged between her thighs making her moan. Fingers dove into her folds, dripping with anticipation of what he promised and what she knew he could do to her. Slick fingertips found their way back to her swollen jewel. She inhaled swiftly, muffling the urge to scream. Reaching behind him, she groped at the muscled wings but jerked her hands back.

Where the hell do I place my hands! I'll pluck him bare at this rate trying to stay quiet!

14

FIRE UP THE NIGHT

Dylan chuckled, his tongue licking the tender salty skin leading to her ear. "My wings are your wings, Angel. One day you'll have your own. Trust me on that one."

I was wild about her before, but the idea she's my opposite even on grounds as a shifter has stripped me of all my doubts. We were made for each other.

"Are we really doing..." She panted. "Doing this?"

Already breathless, are we? So we do like the risk of being caught, don't we Abby?

A huff escaped him. His hands grabbing her hips to bring her to the edge of the roulette table and allowed her to lay back. *Forgive me, I refuse to be gentle this time.* With a confident tug on the front of the halter top, the laces on the back of the dress popped and a breast came free from even the bra. His grin, toothy as he leaned in to suckle at the nipple. Pushing his hip between her parted legs, he slid his hardened length into her wet heat. *We don't have time to take this slow, it's only a matter of*

86

time before he sees us. Sees what he could have had. Sees the devil fucking what once was his angel.

She stifled a moan, tightening on his cock. The sensation sent an enthralling wave through him, and he fought the urge to come. This made his wings flare, only adding to her tightness, adding to her sensation of pleasure. *Shit, she saw that. I better keep her at bay.* Rocking against her, he pulled the full length of his cock in and out, each push making her whimper. The tightening no longer a willing participant to its master. It took everything she had to stifle the yelps and moans, from holding her breath, inhaling deep and swift, to even biting her lip. She tightened and he moaned, another ruffling of his feathers. He pressed hard and deep inside her, lingering there hoping to wait out the teetering edge of his own full orgasm.

Releasing her nipple, Dylan gave her a wide smirk. "If you keep tightening up like that, then we'll have to worry about my loud moaning."

"I'm so afraid…"

"Afraid?" Dylan leaned back, a flash of concern on his face as his wings folded. *Because of me? Because of my shifting?*

"I'm so afraid to touch them." She tightened and the wings flared for her, a laugh escaping her. "And it's kind of fun to see that."

He snorted. "You're hopeless. Here." Pulling her arms off him, he pulled out leaving her whimpering in his wake. "If it bugs you so much," he flipped her with stunning ease. "It's easier to avoid them this way." He tugged her dress up over her ass and to the side, positioning her in doggie-style fashion as his hands roamed her body. "I don't think we've tried this position. Plus, it's cheating if you know when you have me teetering on the edge. I can't have you finishing me off first."

"Dylan, I can't." Her shaken voice came out rushed. "I'll scream."

"Oh? Is this a favorite of yours?" He slid his throbbing cock inside her warmth once more. "You better grab my coat there and muffle yourself. Wouldn't want to have a crowd forming to see you come."

"Dylan I'll squirt..." The rocking of his body connecting with her own sent her scrambling for the jacket to release a squeal into it, muffled and desperate.

I want her to scream.

He maintained his pace, slow and calculated, gauging her body. "Don't you dare hold back. Relax, Angel Abby."

Fingers dug into her hips, rivulets of the rising tide of her orgasm ran hot down her legs. She squeezed her thighs tight, but they were slick as her body arched like a stretching cat. This only made his dick dive deeper inside her pussy. One hand reached out, too short to grip the far edge of the roulette table. He reached out, entwining their fingers and pushed against her harder, grinding and throbbing on the edge of his own orgasm. She began screaming, visceral and alarming as her other arm hugged his coat tighter into her face.

Good girl, give it all to me...

There was a flash of light as she tightened her pussy on his cock, her body shuddering under his. Over his shoulder he locked eyes with the man holding his cell phone. Abigail in the throes of her orgasm hadn't noticed, and with a devilish grin he winked at the pastor still in Sunday attire. With that, he fled through the tarps and Dylan wasted no time turning his attention back to Abigail's peaking. His cock throbbed, his blood rushing, knowing full well who had seen them, who had taken an opportunistic picture and fled without a word.

Ex-fiancé, Pastor Bradley. And my, what a shot he took!

A gush of hot liquid rushed between them, his cock at its peak in Abigail's tight pussy. Unable to resist, he pulled out in a rush, cursing under his breath. Licking his lips, he watched the peach scented liquid dribble down to her ankles. His wings shuddered as he kept a tight hold on his dick, the agonizing tightness of needing to release making his skin crawl. At last, she stopped screaming, a moan all that remained of her orgasm. Reaching over, he stole his coat from her and at last allowed himself to fully come, panting. She rolled to her back, covering her face, legs clamped tight.

"I can't believe we just did that," she whined.

Another laugh escaped him. "I regret nothing. Well, except forgetting a condom. I know better."

"My legs are soaked."

"At least the dress will hide that. My pants look like I pissed myself, but I'm not complaining." He bit his bottom lip, soaking in her body as she lay across the roulette table. "And what makes you think I'm done."

"W-wait!" She tightened her legs.

His hand slipped between, the slickness proving disadvantage as he still found her swollen clit. Frantic, Abigail pulled a swath of her skirt to her mouth and squealed. Humming at each stroke of his finger, slow and steady, coaxing her to open her legs for him. At last, her knees parted wide enough he could kneel between them. His other hand joined, diving inside her and she tightened. Her back arched, knees lifting. All of it allowed his fingers to stroke deeper, rubbing the hot flesh within. Even now, she still dripped and squirted as he pulled her orgasm into a second coming.

Abigail reached down, unsure whether to push him away or pull him into her. Her legs shook, and Dylan licked his lips with anticipation. Shoving her hand to the side, his lips wrapped around her clit. She arched and gave a muffled wail as she pressed the skirt firmly against her mouth. Hungry with want he devoured her, suckling and licking. At last, he gripped her thighs, pushing her open. His tongue dove into the crevasse of her pussy.

Dammit, of all the times not to have a condom in my back pocket!

Juicy and hot, he felt himself growing hard again. Stamina and endurance were trivial when he shifted like this, even on a sexual level he could come again and again without need for reprieve. He ran his tongue up, circling her clit, until she reached down. Moaning, his skin crawled with the thrill of her fingers tangling with his hair and horns. He moaned into her silken heat and her legs jittered, making her join him with her moan.

"D-Dylan..." At first, he refused to stop, but her next words caught his attention. "I found one."

He rocked back on his heels and let her pull herself to a sitting position. She twisted the jacket and out of the pocket, a colorful square wrapper appeared. They grinned at one another, and he wasted no time ripping it open. Rolling it on, she partially hid her face, a mischief and bashful expression. The sparkle in her eyes was worth every bit of the risk of being caught in the act.

Pressing inside her once more, she tightened, and his wings flared. "Dammit."

"That's the worst tell in all gambling history." She repeated the motion, and he puffed out his cheeks unable to stop the ruffling feathers.

"Shut up and fuck me." He wrapped his arms around her, deepening their kiss, lips parting to stroke their tongues.

Grinding hard and fast into her, she synced with his rhythm. Her arms hot against his ribs as they abandoned his jacket. Hands clawed across his back and between the feathered appendages. She moaned into his mouth, another hot gush unfolding as he only continued the rocking of his own hips, peaking. One arm reached to the roulette table, and he realized her amulet had broken and the stone spun off. When they broke the kiss, he paid it more heed and laughed. The glowing stone sat on red nineteen.

"I won."

"You won?" Looking over, she realized what he referred to. "What was the bet against?"

He picked up the stone, now free of the metal backing, and he rolled it over, then laughed. "When we get upstairs, I'll tell you a funny story about your stone."

"Oh!" She plucked it from him and read the words scratched into the back. "Lucius? It's a name!"

"Yea, my name." He kissed her once more, then broke away. "When I was a boy, I tried to give away my devil's luck by putting it into a Devil's Stone. My dad took it, pawned it or chucked it in the trash, who knows. All I know, is that I never saw it again ... until now."

"Wait, then that makes you over two hundred—" Pressing fingers against her lips, he winked as the wings and horns disappeared.

"Dylan's my middle name." He snorted, helping her from the roulette table. "Lucius means *light*. It's the name my mother gave me on a stormy night in 1735. Don't believe all the rumors you hear about me."

To think that bet would lead me to be here with her at this point in time. She was worth the wait.

15

EPILOGUE

Pastor Bradley slipped into the passenger side of a golden Mirage. Pulling out his cell phone, he glared at the photo he'd taken before leaving the casino.

In the driver's seat, the old redhead stared out the car window, confusion written on her face. "Where's Abigail? I thought you found her." Tammy stared at him, but he ignored her. "Pastor Bradley!"

"Shut up!" He snapped, never breaking his glare from his phone.

He brought it closer, picking apart each detail, deciphering which part was his imagination, and the rest, real. Losing sight of Abigail had sent him into a panic attack, spinning in circles from the dizzy casino neon signs. That's when he'd heard voices. He recognized Abigail's.

When the muffled scream unfolded, he pushed through some tarps and froze. There before him, the Devil had been fucking his once beloved fiancée. At first, he locked eyes with the halo above her head. Another moan from her made him realize they were in the throes of passion. He will never erase the image of her, bent over a roulette table, screeching as she reached out. The devil held her down, its wings spread wide, its pointed tail swinging wildly.

He did the only thing he could do; he snapped a photo, using his phone.

The flash went off. Red eyes and a fanged grin looked his way, and he stumbled out. All hope had been lost. The cheating pastor was powerless against a real-life devil. *They never said we'd come face to face with one!* He'd rather save his own soul than throw himself between her and whatever he saw.

"Bradley, where's Abigail?"

"Drive! She's lost to the devil!" Panic filling him, he deleted the picture as she leaned to peek. *If anyone found out I gave an angel to…* "Did you catch her with someone?"

He tossed the phone to the floorboard, disgusted. "Something."

Tammy drove out of the hotel roundabout. "Well, I suppose that's karma."

"You don't understand, Tammy. What I've done, what we did…" He covered his face. "I'm leaving the church. I can't be a pastor. I'm not cut out for this."

This isn't what I signed up for … hell, not even what they trained me to go against. I was to counsel people on normal life problems. Not face demons and devils! Maybe I just imagined it, but that picture…

"What?" Tammy's face flushed. "What about me?"

"Who the fuck cares about you?" He balled his hands on his thighs, his eyes still on the phone. "Far as I know, you were in on the deal."

That's right. She was temptation and I fell for it. I failed the test. I'm not fit to lead a congregation.

"What on earth are you talking about?" she shrieked. "If I recall right, you're the one who put your hand up my skirt!"

"I lied."

"Lied about what?" She marveled, struggling to keep driving in her lane as they reached the busy highway.

"She wanted ... *more* but she's so damn pure... Well, she used to be." He paled, remembering the winged creature. "I settled for you because I was a coward. And because of you, I committed a sin. It's my fault she led herself to the devil!"

For a moment, Tammy grew quiet. The only sound was the rain pattering on the windshield.

"I caught her fucking the Devil, Tammy. Right there in the casino!"

Tammy laughed. "Holy shit, I'm jealous. She upgraded to a billionaire! They say you're lucky if you get the chance to sleep with The Devil at the Saint's Hotel and Casino. Wow, Abigail will have to tell me how she pulled that one off. Now, where do you want to eat?"

Bradley puked on the floorboard.

The End

HONEY CUMMINGS

A passionate, award-winning author of Fantasy, Honey has turned her aim toward erotica. Blending everyday scenarios, and crafting them into steamy, blood-boiling moments for every shade of audience. Whether you want something short and hot, like a student-teacher hook up to the more paranormal flair, where Sleep with Sasquatch has unexpected bonus, look forward to erotic short stories, novellas, and hopefully a Trilogy in the future. Honey's debut erotic short landed at No. 3 in Urban Erotica and continues to satisfy readers time and time again. Be sure to leave her a review and let her know what you think!

amazon.com/Honey-Cummings/e/B07WFX5FDX
AuthorHoneyCummings.com
instagram.com/authorhoneycummings
twitter.com/HoneyCummings2
facebook.com/
Author-Honey-Cummings-101408818012749

More Honey Cummings Books

Sleeping with Sasquatch
Cuddling with Chupacabra
Naked with New Jersey Devil
The Erotic Cryptid Collection

Laying with the Lady in Blue
Wanton Woman in White
Beating it with Bloody Mary
The Erotic Ghosts Collection

Beau and Professor Bestialora
The Goat's Gruff
Goldie and Her Three Beards
Pied Piper's Pipe
Princess Pea's Bed
Pinocchio and the Blow Up Doll
Jack's Beanstalk
Pulling Rapunzel's Hair
The Urban Erotica Fairy Tale
Collection

Curses & Crushes: KU short story

Queen's Incubus: YONDER webnovel

Writing as Valerie Willis

Cedric: The Demonic Knight
Romasanta: Father of Werewolves
The Oracle: Keeper of the Gaea's Gate
Artemis: Eye of Gaea
King Incubus: A New Reign
Queen Succubus: Holder of the Crown

Val's House of Musings: A Mixed Genre Short Story Collection

Writer's Bane: Research 101
Writer's Bane: Formatting

Writing MM Romance as VC Willis

The Prince's Priest
The Priest's Assassin
The Assassin's Saint

The Champion's Lord: YONDER webnovel
Champion's Love: KU short story

MORE BOOKS FROM 4 HORSEMEN PUBLICATIONS

EROTICA

ALI WHIPPE
Office Hours
Tutoring Center
Athletics
Extra Credit
Financial Aid
Bound for Release
Fetish Circuit
Now You See Me
Sexual Playground
Swingers
Discovered
XTC College Series Collection

ARIA SKYLAR
Twisted Eros
Seducing Dionysus

CHASTITY VELDT
Molly in Milwaukee
Irene in Indianapolis
Lydia in Louisville
Natasha in Nashville
Alyssa in Atlanta
Betty in Birmingham
Carrie on Campus
Jackie in Jacksonville
A Humorous Erotica Collection

DALIA LANCE
My Home on Whore Island
Slumming It on Slut Street
Training of the Tramp
The Imperfect Perfection
Spring Break
72% Match
It Was Meant To Be... Or Whatever

NICK SAVAGE
The Fairlane Incidents
The Fortunate Finn Fairlane
The Fragile Finn Fairlane
The Complete Package

LGBT Erotica

Dominic N. Ashen
Steel & Thunder
Storms & Sacrifice
Secrets & Spires
Arenas & Monsters
My Three Orc Dads: a Novella
Before the Storm: a Novella

Eskay Kabba
Hidden Love
Not So Hidden
Signs of Affection
Deeply Devoted to Him
Honest Love
A Plane and Simple Connection

Grayson Ace
How I Got Here
First Year Out of the Closet
You're Only a Top?
You're Only a Bottom?
I Think I'm a Serial Swiper
Lookin in All the Wrong Places
What Makes Me a Whore?
A Breach in Confidentiality
Back Door Pass
My European Adventure
An Unexpected Affair
Finding True Love
The Dr. Cage Chronicles

Leo Sparx
Before Alexander
Claiming Alexander
Taming Alexander
Saving Alexander
The Fall of the House of Otter
The Case of Armando

Robert Lewis
Someone to Love
Someone to Come Home To
Someone to Kiss

Discover more at
4HorsemenPublications.com